The BOOB GIRLS

The Burned Out Old Broads Table 12

in Lies, Spies and Cinnamon Rolls

A Novel by Joy Johnson

Copyright ©2010 Joy Johnson

ISBN: 1-56123-217-3

Library of Congress information on file.

GRIEF ILLUSTRATED PRESS

PO Box 4600
Omaha, NE 68104

Order from: www.theboobgirls.com
1-866-218-0101
centeringcorp@aol.com

Cover design by Janet Sieff, Centering Corporation

The BOOB Girls Two

The Burned Out Old Broads
at Table 12
In Lies, Spies and Cinnamon Rolls

A Novel by Joy Johnson
Editor / Designer: Janet Sieff

In memory of Terry Roberts,

great friend, sweet companion and good man.

And because he loved dogs, this can also be for
Bailey and Hershel.

Part One

It's A Knick-Knack
Patty Whack

I love cinnamon rolls.
They just melt in your mouth and leave a high-
calorie taste.
Dr. Robinson Leary

*I don't care. Even if they **are** wrapped in plastic,*
The calories slip through and slide onto your hips.
Mary Rose McGill

Cinnamon rolls are comfort food.
When was the last time you heard someone say,
"I'm stressed. Let's go have salad."
Hadley Joy Morris-Whitfield

So much has been said and sung of beautiful young
girls, why doesn't somebody wake up to the beauty
of old women? Harriet Beecher Stowe

Friendship – Friendship – What A Perfect Blendship

Patty Whack was just no fun at all. She had come to Meadow Lakes Retirement Community in Omaha, Nebraska, just before Christmas, plain as a brown chicken and dragging a black bag big enough to hold a medium-sized dog. She had plopped her skinny butt down in the chair at table 12 that used to belong to Maggie Patten. Maggie, the very one who had named them The BOOB Girls, The Burned Out Old Broads, and now this new, unpleasant woman had caused them to stop laughing, stop making jokes and stop kidding each other when they were at table 12.

She was like the Devil walking out of a Tarot deck.

She was like a rainy weekend at Disney World.

She was like your great-aunt Matilda with garlic breath.

They didn't like her.

She was no Maggie Patten.

Maggie Patten had been a bow-legged, feisty, bossy, risk-taking retired rancher with minimum-maintenance hair from the Sand Hills of western Nebraska, that beautiful area where wagon trains had passed by Chimney Rock and used the Platte River for their supply of food and water on their way to the Rocky Mountains and beyond.

But Maggie Patten was dead. She had taught them how to drive a Hummer pulling a good-sized trailer, been the leader when they lived out every woman's fantasy and left with no forwarding address. They had headed west, loved the boys at The Ragged Ass Saloon and gotten tiny daisy tattoos together.

And now their Maggie was dead. And now they were thinking it would be a pleasure to accord Patty Whack the same privilege.

"She's a damn wet blanket," Hadley Joy Morris-Whitfield said. They were sitting alone at table 12, their spot in the spacious and gracious dining room at Meadow Lakes. Spring was peeking in through the floor-to-ceiling windows. Hadley had been a socialite of sorts. She had liked big men, big dogs and big cars. Her big husband, who had not always been the most faithful, but had always been the most loving, had died in a fiery plane crash; a private plane, of course. Now Hadley, who was nearly six feet tall with thick white hair that reminded people of the old Vidal Sassoon ad, was sitting with her legs crossed looking at her table mates. She had on a Nebraska Cornhuskers sweatshirt and jeans and she was drumming her fingers on the table. It was annoying.

"Piss, moan, bitch," Robinson Leary said. Robbie Leary was *Dr.* Leary, a retired English professor from Creighton University. Her husband, a long-time multiple sclerosis patient, had been a professor as well, and they had lived a good life in a trendy apartment in Omaha's trendy Old Market where the streets were still brick and petunias hung from the tops of wooden awnings reaching to the curbs.

Robinson Leary, with skin the color of a rich latte, her hair salt and pepper, was half black, half Cajun.

7

She liked spicy food, good poetry and mindless mystery novels. She sat with one leg under her, a Creighton Bluejays jogging suit fitting her easily and comfortably.

"We don't have any fun when she's around," Mary Rose McGill said. "And she looks worse than I did when I came here." Mary Rose had been dowdy and shy when she first sat down at table 12, but she had been loved into becoming a butterfly, breaking out of her cocoon until now she was beautiful. Her yellow pantsuit (fifty percent off at Target) complimented her blonde hair, styled by Peyton Claireborne, breathtaking drag queen and master hair stylist. While all three wore glasses on occasion, Mary Rose was the one who had bright red frames. Her husband, who had pretty much ignored her while he was alive (and pretty much still did while he was dead) would definitely have noticed her now and would have probably been afraid of her. She had lost sixty pounds, found her voice and found what real friendship meant as well, the kind that arrives softly and embraces the soul.

The BOOB Girls had a bond that only women appreciate. They could say anything. As some psychologists have defined it; they were *real*. They knew each other, loved each other, cared for each other, and no one had to pretend or show a false face or be anyone other than just who she really was. But now there was this fourth woman who even after a few months hardly talked to them, whose presence sat on table 12 like a mildewed tablecloth with wrinkles.

Patty Whack even looked like a mildewed tablecloth with wrinkles. The plain, secretive little woman had begged off sharing Christmas dinner with them in Hadley's luxury third floor apartment, consistently arrived late for meals, ate in a hurry then vanished – sometimes when none of them were looking. She was quiet, homely and sullen. Being around her was uncomfortable. Her ugly hair was gun-metal gray, pulled back in a tight bun at the nape of her neck. She wore old-fashioned house dresses in floral prints, had two sweaters, one blue, one white, and two pairs of ugly shoes, one pair black, one pair brown. Her right wrist sported a big god-awful watch, so ugly it would be ashamed to be seen at some shyster's rip-off table on a New York City street corner. Ugly, ugly, ugly.

The three girls were pretty much alone in the dining room now. Wiley Vondra, the cowboy-wanna-be was wearing his usual brown leather vest and cowboy boots and playing cards with three other men close by and two women were enjoying early afternoon coffee at a table near one of the hallways.

Hadley suddenly sat up straight, reached over and touched her friends' arms. "Look!" She pointed to a spot just past Wiley. A huge yellow cat skidded around the table, paws sliding and scratching on the tile floor. She was trying to make the turn so fast her fluffy side was nearly touching the tiles. She was scrambling and clawing her way to an upright position, her feet trying to find purchase in mid-air. Immediately behind her was a huge, tall man running as fast as he could in a squat position.

10

"He looks like a duck," Robbie said.

Mary Rose stood to see better. "More like a turkey."

"He looks like Sasquatch," Hadley said.

The man was wearing a plaid flannel shirt, baggy black jeans and high-top sneakers. A mass of white hair flew in all directions on his head. He must have weighed nearly three hundred pounds and if he ever got out of his crouch, he would stand at least six feet four inches tall.

He was gaining on the cat, who scrambled for her balance, found it, got a head start and leaped onto the lap of one of the ladies sitting at the other table. "Yeeee!," the lady said, and the cat settled into her lap, turned toward the Sasquatch, bared one paw and hissed. The big man didn't break stride. Still in a running squat, he zoomed by the lady, grabbed the cat in one sweeping move, tucked it under his arm, made a slight turn and dashed through the swinging doors leading into the ladies bathroom. The dining room became totally quiet.

"Took a wrong turn there," Wiley said. In just seconds the big man, still running in a crouch, cat tucked securely under his arm like a football, dashed out of the ladies room and into the hallway leading from the dining room.

Everyone leaned out of their chairs and peered down the hall. After a few steps, the big man stood up, put his hand over the cat's eyes so it couldn't see and try to escape and headed down the hall. Coming toward him was a lady even larger than man and cat. She met him, rubbed the cat's ears then reached up and planted a kiss on the man's cheek. Still upright, he moved down the hall and the woman headed toward the dining room.

Evangeline Goldberg

People usually heard Evangeline Goldberg before they saw her. She thundered into the dining room, her massive frame swaying from side to side. Every step made the floor shake and the small group left at the tables looked up at her in one single motion.

Here was a force with which to be reckoned. She was dressed in a model's house coat dress that could have been made by Omaha Tent and Awning. Her neck and thighs made any NFL linebacker look like a wimp. Her hair was in tiny, springy gray curls which had once been tightly held down by bobby pins and made her look like a character out of a cartoon. The only footwear anyone had seen on Mrs. Goldberg were crocheted house slippers with pom-poms on the toes.

Today the dress was pink, the slippers were pink and covering her middle was an apron with the day of the week embroidered across the front. Today was Tuesday, but Mrs. Goldberg's apron was boldly trying to convince everyone it was Friday. She was carrying a basket covered with pink gingham and sporting a tasteful pink bow. The contents were even more tasteful. Evangeline Goldberg made the best cinnamon rolls in the world. No contest. As she moved past the small group in the dining room, their noses lifted. They breathed deeply.

It took her awhile to get to the girls' table, and when she did she stopped, puffed a little, pulled out the empty chair. "Hello girls," she bellowed and plopped the basket of rolls down in the middle of table 12. Hadley, Robbie and Mary Rose took deep, delicious breaths and glanced at the basket.

"Mrs. Goldberg," Hadley said. "Please sit down." Mrs. Goldberg's sitting down was an act worth paying to see. She oozed into the chair, with parts of her body slipping out between the seat and the arms. She puffed and huffed and settled in with the help of gravity and supernatural faith.

"Was that your cat, Mrs. Goldberg?" Hadley asked.
"Oh yes, dear," Mrs. Goldberg said. "That would be Margaret Thatcher. Excuse my language, but she is such a bitch."
"Cat or prime minister?" Hadley smiled.
Mrs. Goldberg smiled back, a twinkle in her eye.
"Yes," she said.
"And the man who caught her?" Robbie asked.

"That would be the nephew of my dearly-departed husband, Eli. His name is Rueben. He and his three brothers just moved into the apartment next to mine. They're wonderful boys." She paused and smiled a sad smile. "Wonderful boys. Different fathers."

"Are they all Jewish like you, Mrs. Goldberg?" Mary Rose asked. Mary Rose described herself as a recovering Catholic. Her husband had been extremely loyal to the church, attending mass every day of the year. He had suffered a massive stroke during one service and died a few days later.

"Oh, my dear," Mrs. Goldberg said, shaking her curls. "I'm not Jewish."
"Oh, I'm sorry," Mary Rose said. "I just assumed with a name like Goldberg..."
"That would be Eli, dear. I never converted though I respected the faith and we kept the traditions. No," she shook her head. "I'm Baptist. But from the Jewish side of the family I did learn the four great religious truths." She smiled a wicked smile, raised

her right hand to count on her fingers and said in a conspiratorial voice:

"Palestinians do not recognize Jewish rights to the Holy Land.

Jews do not recognize Jesus as the Messiah.

Protestants do not recognize the Pope as their religious leader.

And Baptists do not recognize each other at Hooters."

And she hooted another loud laugh. The girls joined in. The two ladies having coffee had left, but Wiley turned toward them from where he sat, still playing cards, and grinned a wide, funny grin.

There was a moment of silence and Robbie smiled a gentle smile. "How are you, Mrs. Goldberg?"

"Oh...sick, tired and run down," Mrs. Goldberg replied. "But I'm lucky." She rubbed the bump that was nearly lost under her triple chins. "I have this goiter, but it doesn't give me any grief. Now my Aunt Elsie had a goiter so big she could have worn bras with three cups." Mrs. Goldberg roared with

laughter again and the girls laughed with her and
looked harder at her goiter and then at the basket of
rolls. "I have the normal aches and pains for a lady
my age, but I say just because you *have* a pain
doesn't mean you have to *be* one."

She took a deep breath, "But I didn't come here to
talk about my health," she said. "I'm on a mission.
I've noticed you've had trouble with that little short
lady who joined you a few months ago." She
pointed to the basket of rolls. "You take those to
her and have a heart-to-heart talk, you hear? You
three have history together. You're best friends.
Anyone trying to be part of your friendship will be
an outsider until you let her know you want her, and
my rolls have won more friends than free cheese.
You each have one, too. Portions here are so small
they wouldn't satisfy a canary." Mrs. Goldberg
should know; she had a canary.

"Now I gotta go." Mrs. Goldberg sighed. "I have
another batch ready for the oven and Herman needs
feeding." Mrs. Goldberg leaned forward, planted

her feet on the floor, put her hands on the chair arms
and pushed as hard as she could. Robbie and Mary
Rose reached over and pushed down on the chair
arms and Mrs. Goldberg rose up and oozed back out
of the chair, nodded to the girls then thundered
across the dining room toward the hallway.

"Who's Herman?" Mary Rose asked.

"Probably her canary," Hadley said. She was
looking at the cinnamon rolls.

"We do NOT need to eat these!" Mary Rose said.
She was looking at them, too.

"Yes we do," Robbie and Hadley said together.

All three reached for a roll at the same time.

"Remember that old saying, 'Inside me is a skinny
woman screaming to get out?' Well in this case we
can shut her up with a cinnamon roll." Hadley took
the first good-sized bite. The taste of almond and
butter melted in her mouth.

The card game at Wiley Vondra's table broke up
and he sauntered over, stopped at the table, reached
into the basket and grabbed a roll. He winked at

Mary Rose, nodded to Hadley and Robbie and continued to mosey on toward the entrance to his wing.

Wiley was rugged and weathered in a soft kind of way. He was about an inch taller than Hadley, thin and amiable. He had a reputation at Meadow Lakes because it was widely known that at midnight on the fifteenth of every month he went to the laundry room, stripped down to only his brown leather vest, cowboy boots and beat-up old Stetson and played solitaire bare-assed naked. When Wiley Vondra did his laundry, Wiley Vondra did *all* his laundry. On occasion Wiley invited the girls at table 12 down to the laundry room for a friendly midnight game of poker. On occasion three of them accepted. Patty Whack, of course, never joined them for anything.

"Oh well," Hadley said. "Let's take the friggin' rolls to our Ms. Whack. It won't hurt."

19

The Man in Patty's Apartment

It was late afternoon by the time they were ready to visit Patty. They had driven to the Hy-Vee Grocery store and picked out a small bouquet of daisies.

"We haven't decided what to say," Mary Rose said.

"We just play it by ear," Robbie replied.

"We'll try our best," Mary Rose sighed.

"Trying is an activity in and of itself," Hadley said.

"We will *do* it." Her tone was not at all convincing.

As they stepped into the sun, Mary Rose said in a soft voice, "SHIT." It wasn't the common "S" word. It was their signal to watch their posture. **S**houlders straight, **H**ead high, **E**yes (**I**) straight ahead, glancing down and **T**ummy tucked in. They straightened up and walked tall.

The afternoon was cool with a breeze blowing through the still-barren trees in the big back lawn. Later in the spring a fountain would flow with gentle sounds near the gazebo which was a perfect place for reading, relaxing and meeting friends. They decided it would be friendlier to walk across the lawn and approach Patty's apartment through the sliding glass patio doors instead of going down the hall, ringing her doorbell and looking like ancient Girl Scouts peddling cinnamon rolls.

Clouds had moved in as they approached Patty's apartment, and without a reflection from the sun, they could see clearly through the glass doors and into the living room. Hadley suddenly stopped short. "Look," she said, pointing to the glass doors "There's a man in Patty's apartment," She leaned forward and squinted. "That's not all."

"He has a gun," Robbie gasped, leaning forward and squinting along with her. They stopped in their tracks and stared.

A tall man in a dark suit was standing with his back to them. Patty Whack stood in front of him, her hands in the air.

"Who do we call?" Mary Rose asked.

"Not Ghostbusters, that's for sure," Hadley said.

Robbie straightened up. "We don't have time to call anyone. We have to help her ourselves."

"You think this is some kind of girl thing?" Hadley asked, sounding hesitant.

Robbie nodded and Mary Rose gripped the basket tighter. They walked on tip-toe, though the ground would have muffled the sound of their footsteps even if they were running. They sneaked and crept until they were within an arm's length of the sliding door. Inside the man was waving his gun, and they could hear his angry voice yelling.

"What if it's locked?" Mary Rose whispered.

"It isn't," Robbie whispered back and she pointed to the side of the door that stood open half an inch.

"On the count of three we pull the door, crash in and take him down."

"Yeah, right," Hadley said.

They could see Patty looking over the man's shoulder, her eyes wide. She was shaking her head ever so slightly, signaling for them not to come in.

"One," Hadley said.

"Two," Robbie said.

"Three!" Mary Rose yelled and she slid open the sliding door so hard it banged and bounced. At the same time she reached into the basket, grabbed a cinnamon roll and threw it at the man's head. He turned to see what the commotion was and the roll hit him in the eye. "Hey!" he yipped.

Robbie grabbed a roll and got the other eye. "Hey!" the man said again. As he turned away from Robbie's roll smash, Mary Rose jammed the bouquet of flowers into his mouth. He yelled a muffled, "Shmay!" again.

"They never have much of a vocabulary," Robbie said as Hadley grabbed a lamp from an end table and smashed it over his head. He was still gripping the gun, but frosting was on both eyebrows and his eyelashes and he was trying to rub his eyes with the coat sleeve of his free arm while he pulled flowers from his mouth. "Hey!" he snarled again.
"Very repetitious," Mary Rose said and she gave him her famous groin kick, missed as usual and

dislocated his kneecap.

From out of nowhere came a karate yell, and two feet flew through the air, hitting the man in the head as he tried to grab his injured knee. He dropped to the other knee, yelling in pain, and the two feet were in the air again, hitting the side of his head with tremendous force. The gun spun out of reach. The man crashed onto his back and was still.

They stood looking at his prone figure, spread-eagled flat on the floor. They were panting as if they'd just finished a marathon. Then the man twitched and groaned.

"He's waking up!" Mary Rose said.

"Quick," Hadley said, "sit on him."

She gingerly sat on his chest just under his chin. Robbie hurried to the other side and took her seat on his stomach. Mary Rose plopped down hard on his abdomen. A long, loud stream of foul-smelling gas escaped his butt. It sounded like two dozen balloons releasing their air at the same time and lasted a good five seconds. All three women's eyebrows shot up.

"Eueww!" Mary Rose said.

"Whew!" Robbie said.

Hadley covered her nose and fanned the air in front of her. Then they heard a low growl.

"Fart of the century," the voice said. And for the first time since they had known her, the woman who called herself Patty Whack was almost smiling. The wig, which had been her dull gray hair, lay on the floor, a bun still secure at the neck. This woman had a white burr cut.

"She's wearing a body suit!" Mary Rose said.

Still almost smiling, the new personality opened up the huge, clumsy-looking watch she always wore and said into it, "38B here. I need a clean-up." Then she snapped the watch closed, looked at the girls staring at her, mouths still gaping and said, "Hang around ladies, we'll have some coffee."

Ignoring them, the Patty Whack person walked to

an end table, pulled her ugly black bag out from under it, squatted beside it, opened it and pulled out a large syringe filled with a white fluid. She walked to the prone figure on the floor, stuck the needle into his neck and emptied the syringe. They gasped a communal gasp and the woman looked up. "What?! This will just keep him quiet for a while." Her clunky shoes looked even chunkier and strange with her black athletic wear. Her short-sleeved black tee seemed to be one piece with her black shorts. What they had once thought were old-fashioned cotton stockings were really tights and the muscles in her arms and legs stood out and were very defined.

"She has no body fat," Mary Rose whispered.

"No wonder we didn't like her," Hadley said.

Calamity Doodles

The athletic little figure put the syringe back into her bag as carefully as any nurse, looked at the three women and motioned to a table in the efficient little kitchen.

"I don't have decaf," she said.

Hadley did an eye roll. "Who cares?"

"Robbie agreed. "One cup won't hurt me," An atrial flutter kept Robbie off caffeine and alcohol, but she figured her adrenaline was so high it would cancel out the stimulant, like drinking a Diet Coke while eating a cookie cancels the calories in the cookie.

Mary Rose leaned in toward the other two. "That woman is *not* a 38B," she whispered. "I'm a 34B and she doesn't have the boobs I have."

"I don't think it's a bra size," Robbie whispered. "It's a code name. She's either with a government agency or the cops." Hadley looked at her and did another eye roll. Robbie shrugged. "I read a lot of mysteries," she said.

The sliding glass doors opened and three men in black slipped in, bringing dusk and long shadows in with them. In the dim light they looked like menacing silhouettes against the white walls.

The first, an attractive African-American, knelt and put a stethoscope to the chest of the still figure on the floor. The second was Hispanic. He walked toward the little woman standing by the coffee pot and held out a small computer-like machine. She pressed her finger onto the screen and he pocketed the gadget. The third man, a Caucasian was built like Max Starks, offensive tackle for the Pittsburg Steelers. The big man grabbed their victim under the arms, lifted him into the air, slung him over his shoulder and led the way out the door and into the shadows. No one had spoken a word.

"You came at a rather awkward time," Patty Whack said. And she sat down in the fourth chair, tucking one leg under her. "I'm not really Patty Whack."

"No kidding," Hadley said. The coffee was dripping, smelling good and nearly ready to drink.

"Wait a minute," the woman said. She stood and went into the living room and picked up the basket that had carried the cinnamon rolls the girls had turned into deadly weapons. She brought it to the table, grabbed some napkins off the counter and captured a knife from a small drawer. There were three rolls left in the basket and the woman deftly cut them into fourths sticking a piece in her mouth.

"I love these things," she said, but since there was a lot of cinnamon roll in her mouth, it came out as, "Yi muff eig dings," They stared at her. She turned, grabbed four mugs from an old-fashioned mug tree sitting by the sink, slammed them onto the table, reached for the coffee pot and began to pour.

"I work for an agency whose job is to protect America," she began. She placed the coffee pot on the table beside the basket, sat down and tucked one leg under her like before.

"See?" Robbie said. Hadley did an eye roll.
"My name is Calamity Doodles."
Hadley couldn't help herself. She laughed.
Calamity Doodles glared at her.
"Sorry," Hadley said, "nervous habit." Mary Rose began to giggle and Robbie started to snicker. The

29

woman across from them almost smiled once more. They sipped their coffee.

"I grew up in the circus. My father was the star clown, Doodles. My mother was star of the circus Wild West show. She was a sharp shooter and trick rider, so I have my dad's name and a Calamity Jane heritage." She looked toward the ceiling. "There wasn't the opportunity for women in those days," she sighed. "Today my mother could be a sniper or even an assassin." The girls stared at her and were quiet. "She could even go into politics," she said.

Robbie frowned. "But you didn't keep your real name when you came here."
"No," Calamity said. "I'm under cover here."
Mary Rose leaned toward her.
"There's a microchip somewhere here in Omaha that has the names of an entire company of United States secret agents, and right now it's on its way to the bad guys. It's stalled here because the courier was shot and killed. My job is to find *it* before *they*

find some other delivery boy or girl."

"I love spy talk," Mary Rose said.

"So who was the man in the suit holding a gun on you?" Hadley asked.

"That was George, my fifth husband." They stared at her. Mary Rose held up one hand and spread her fingers, "*Fifth* husband?" she said.

"Right, all my men were with the agency. Number one was shot by a bad guy who was lying on the ground. Bullet went through his butt and into his heart. Freak thing. Number two jumped off a bridge after we had a fight, but I know he was pushed." Somehow Robbie had no problem imagining a man married to a karate queen with a mean temper jumping off a bridge. Calamity looked around the room. "Number three just disappeared." Robbie could imagine that, too. "Number four was shot as well."

"By the same bad guys?" Mary Rose asked,

"Nope. Jealous husband."

"And George was number five." Hadley clarified.

"Is there a number six?"

"Oh yeah," Calamity nodded. "He's out to kill me, too. Five and six went over to the dark side. Henry, the sixth, will try to kill me, too."

"There's not a Henry the eighth is there?" Hadley said. Calamity just looked at her.

"If all these men are out to kill you, why don't you run?" Hadley asked. "Get another identity?"

"It's my job," Calamity said. "We want to find out where the chip is. The only way to do that is if George talks or Henry comes to share a cinnamon roll now that they know where I am."

"But Patty…, I mean, Calamity, that means your life is in danger," Robbie said.

Calamity almost smiled again. "I was a clown in the circus from the time I could walk, and I was in my mother's Wild West show. My life has always been in danger, Professor."

There were a few minutes of silence. Then Mary Rose spoke. "But how did you pick a name like

Patty Whack? Is it a code name or something?"
Calamity's upper lip curled up just a tad. "No. It's
from my favorite joke when I was in junior high.
See, there was this frog that walked into a bank and
went up to a teller. The teller was a pretty young
thing, and her name tag read, 'Patricia Whack.' So
the frog says, 'Ms. Whack, my name is Kermit
Jagger and I need a loan.' Ms. Whack looks at the
frog and says, 'I'm sorry sir. We can't give you a
loan unless you have an account here.' The frog
pulls out a tiny little statue of a gold guitar, hands it
to her and says, 'Give this to your bank president
and tell him my name. He'll give me the loan.' So
Patricia Whack goes into the president's office and
says, 'Sir, there's a frog outside. He says his name
is Kermit Jagger. He wants a loan and doesn't have
an account, but he said to tell you his name and give
you this.' She hands him the little statue and says,
'But Sir, what is it?' The bank president takes it,
looks at it and says..." Calamity looked around the
table... "Are you ready? 'It's a knick-knack Patty
Whack. Give the frog a loan. His old man's a

Rolling Stone.'"

Hadley chuckled and Robbie smiled. "I like it."

Mary Rose frowned. "I don't get it".

Mick Jagger," Robbie explained. "From the
Rolling Stones band and the old nursery rhyme,
'Knick knack patty whack give the dog a bone. This
old man came rolling home.'" Robbie was on a roll
herself..."Remember *Jumpin' Jack Flash*? Sir Mick
is thin, wears leather jackets, skin-tight jeans and
has really cute buns.

"Oh!" Mary Rose said. "*Him!*"

Getting to Know You

Calamity Doodles turned out to be okay after all.
She seemed to like the girls. She seldom smiled and
never laughed. They could tell she had never been
really close to anyone. It seemed she wanted to
belong and couldn't allow herself to move into the
belonging.

All too many people present a picture to the outside
world that looks like the traditional Christmas letter;

all good news and cheeriness, pretended pride in children and jobs, whitewashing the toil and grind and sorrow that come naturally with life. The BOOB Girls didn't have to pretend. They didn't have to fake it. When one was asked, "How are you?" she didn't have to have a smile on a stick to hold in front of her face and say, "fine," a four-letter word when you're burdened with troubles and grief.

When Mary Rose's daughters ignored her, she bitched about it. When Hadley's son divorced his pencil-thin third wife, Hadley cried with them. If Robbie had to be taken to the emergency room when her heart went out of rhythm, they drove her there, stayed with her and went out to lunch when she was discharged. As for Calamity, she listened, nodded, patted hands but told them almost nothing about herself. She remained a mystery.

One day she came to Table 12 bearing gifts. She sat down with the other three, fished around in her pocket and pulled out four tiny little silver angels.

"Here you go, girls," she said. "I never did thank you for the cinnamon rolls." They all laughed and slipped the little angels into their pockets. It was the nicest thing Calamity would ever do for them.

And Calamity went with them now and then. It was a perfect spring day when they walked across the Bob Kerrey Pedestrian Bridge, a three thousand foot span that linked Omaha, Nebraska, to its sister city across the Missouri River, Council Bluffs, Iowa.

The bridge was beautiful, with towers and lights and areas where walkers could pause to watch the rushing waters of the great river as it surged its way toward St. Louis. Not far from the bridge was the site where wagon trains ferried across the river and headed west. Those wagons would cross the Nebraska plains and witness the great migration of the Sand Hill Cranes, ducks, geese and whooping cranes.

Bob Kerrey, after whom the bridge was named, was

a former Senator and Governor of Nebraska and his opposition claimed Nebraskans had a love affair with Bob Kerrey. Bob Kerrey, on the other hand, had a love affair with actress Debra Winger when she filmed *Terms of Endearment* in Nebraska. Bob Kerrey was not a boring politician.

Other walkers on the bridge nodded and smiled when they met. A little boy eight or nine years old smiled and gave them a cheery wave. Hadley laughed. "When my David was that age he was playing with Scotty, our neighbor boy and all at once he came running into the house. 'Mommy!' he said, 'what is it called when two people sleep in the same bedroom and one is on top of the other?'" "I thought *teachable moment,* so I sat down and told him all about sex – in detail. He nodded and jumped down and fifteen minutes later he came running back in. 'Mommy! It's called *bunk beds,* and Scotty's mother wants to talk to you.'"
They all smiled. "And...?" Robbie said.
Hadley turned toward them, a big smile on her face.

"Scotty's mom was pouring the champagne when I got there. She had no idea how to do the sex talk and she was as grateful as a good bottle of bubbly that I'd done it for her." They laughed again.

Hadley pointed. A flock of black birds swooped over the bridge and into the trees on the Iowa side. "People used to try to get more beautiful birds at their feeders and didn't want starlings, but my mother said she would always feed the little sparrows and the starlings because they stayed with us all winter."

Robbie watched the flock for a minute. "I don't know who said it, but there's a beautiful statement about always having winter and always having rain, but there will come a day when the birds fly north again. It talks about hope coming back and the cycle of life." And they married their way on across the bridge like the Tinman, the Scarecrow and the Cowardly Lion. Calamity was short enough to be Dorothy.

Ralph "Percolator" Rasmussen

The one activity no one at Meadow Lakes missed was birthday parties. They had no choice. Birthdays were celebrated during lunch, so unless you weren't eating you were cornered. "Date of Birth" was on every application and contract so you were stuck again; they had your date. Your name and age were announced to the entire dining room; cake was served *before* the meal so there would be no sneaking out early. The one consolation was the cake was delicious.

The girls were sitting outside at one of the patio tables drinking iced tea when one of the homelier men in the complex came into view. He was tall and skinny with no butt or belly. His hair was thin and wispy with tinges of red mixed in with the gray. His big-boned face was so marred with ancient acne scars that he looked like he'd taken a shotgun blast head-on. The ugliest part of him however, was that he was just plain mean. He was carrying a coffee mug with a picture of Grumpy the dwarf on it.

No one knew what Ralph ("Percolator") Rasmussen had done during his working days. Some said he was an accountant, some a lawyer and one rumor had him as a wrestler who'd lost too much weight and muscle fooling around with too many loose women. He wasn't the sharpest knife in the drawer and another rumor said his mind had started to go south about the time he reached puberty. His nickname, "Percolator," fit because he made random sounds exactly like his coffee maker.

"Interesting, those coffee maker sounds," Robbie said as Ralph came up the walk. "Maybe he's just lived with his coffee maker for so long they started to sound like each other like old married people."

Hadley nodded. "I sometimes snore softly like my electric can opener."
Ralph walked by the girls' table, snarled and percolated something like, "dumb bitches."
"Hey!" Calamity shouted. "Watch it, Perky!"
The girls looked at her. So did Ralph the Percolator.

"I can say whatever I want to, Bitchy Witch," Ralph snarled and perked again.

"Ha!" Calamity said. "Hardy Har Har, Ralphie. I bet you we can just look at you and tell how old you are." Hadley, Mary Rose and Robbie looked from Calamity to Ralph and back again.

"Can not!" Ralph said.

"Can too!" Calamity snorted. "But you have to do what we say."

"Like what?" He percolated again.

"Drop your pants and drawers and jump around in a circle three times."

The girls raised their eyebrows, looked at Calamity again and smiled innocent-looking smiles.

"I'm not doin' that for nobody," Ralph said.

Calamity smiled. "OK, then admit we win."

"No way! No bitch can outsmart the Percolator." Ralph put his coffee mug on the ground, unbuckled his belt, pulled down his zipper and dropped his pants around his ankles. He was wearing bright green boxers with white palm trees and turtles on them. One turtle was located in a strategic spot on the front. He rumbled at the girls and dropped his shorts. He took a deep breath and danced and jumped around in a tight circle three times, dragging his pants and shorts with him.

"That was good Ralph," Calamity said. "Now face the other way and give us a full moon, Honey." Ralph glared at them. They smiled at Ralph. He turned, and mooned them. They applauded.

"Pull 'em up, Ralphie," Calamity said.

Ralphie pulled 'em up, zipped and buckled. He grinned an ugly grin and glared at Calamity.

"You're 84," she announced. Ralph looked surprised and made a furtive glance at his crotch.

"How could you tell that just by looking at my junk?" He was glaring harder at them.

Calamity looked at the girls and pointed to Mary Rose who smiled and nodded. "We were at your birthday party last week," she said.

"Shit!" Ralph said. He picked up his cup and walked off, making a whistling sound followed by a beep – like a coffee maker makes when it's done.

"He wears boxers," Mary Rose giggled.

"It wasn't nice, but Ralph deserves it," Hadley said. She thought for a second. "Geez, I hope no one saw us. He could have been arrested for exposing himself." They looked back toward the Meadow Lakes office windows. Jane, one of the managers, was standing at the window, grinning from ear to ear and giving them two thumbs up.

"Actually, Ralph was pretty well endowed," Hadley said. "He had a good-sized winkie there."

"It was indeed a fine dickey-doo," Calamity added.

"An impressive tallywacker," Robbie said and looked at Mary Rose.

Mary Rose hiccupped and smiled. Her smile got wider and she started to laugh. "I haven't heard tallywacker for years," Then she broke into loud guffaws of laughter. They waited and watched her.

Finally, through tears of laughter she said, "When I was a teenager I heard an evangelist. He spent one long sermon trying to prove that God was male, and all I could think of," she wiped her eyes with her sleeve, "was this huge old man with a white beard jumping around Heaven from cloud to cloud with his tallywacker bouncing up and down and spinning in circles." Tears were running down her cheeks. "Were the tallywhacker circles clockwise or counter-clockwise," Calamity asked.

Mary Rose thought for a minute, the image coming back to her. She spun her finger in a tight circle to help her remember. "Definitely clockwise," she giggled and nodded. "Definitely clockwise."

Suddenly Mary Rose jumped up. "I've got to go pee!" And she nearly ran toward the nearest door.

Part Two

The BOOB Boys

The Burned Out Old Bastards

The Lord shall provide and they shall be called
Cinnamon Rolls
Robert: retired minister, while holding up Bible

The thing I like about dictators is
they never nag you about smoking or eating
cinnamon rolls.
Rueben: life-time of heavy labor

Silence

Leonard (doesn't speak)

I like Aunt Evangeline's rolls with nuts in them best.
They remind me of our family.
Clyde: retired computer programmer

A woman over 50 will never wake you in the middle
of the night and ask, 'What are you thinking?' She
doesn't care what you think. Andy Roone

Every so often Calamity would disappear for a few days. Each time she left a note under one of their doors saying she would be back soon and not to worry. The notes were never signed. They had an idea that not many people had ever worried about Calamity and they felt it their privilege to do so.

And sure enough, in a few days Calamity would appear at table 12 as if nothing had happened. Sometimes she looked tired. Once she had a large bruise on her cheek. Each time she returned, for the first two or three days, the wiry little spy kept the big black bag close beside her. The other three girls always acted as if she had never been away at all. She joined them for poker in the laundry room with Wiley and always won. She credited it to a lot of down time in the circus. She walked with them as the weather warmed and they made trips to the cemetery where their husbands were buried.

Robbie, whose husband had been the love of her life, frequently had TUGS, Totally Unexpected

Grief Surges, which came when she heard his favorite song, saw someone who looked like him, walked by a vacant wheelchair or visited a place they had gone together. The cemetery was a sanctuary where she could shed tears and talk about their life together.

There was just the slightest mist as they made their way to the grave of Maggie Patten's husband. It was suspected that Maggie had poisoned him, but no one would ever know since his ashes were in the ground and Maggie was in the Pacific Ocean. Mary Rose carried a bouquet of flowers from the Hy-Vee Grocery store and they stood in front of the headstone looking at the chipped surface where Maggie had drilled five shots from her father's old Colt 45 and had never visited the grave during their cemetery visits. Mary Rose laid a flower on the stone, not to honor the husband, but as a tribute to Maggie's spunk, her accuracy with the old colt and the love they had for her.

Mary Rose's husband's grave was next. She laid a daisy in front of his stone and said, "At one time you could have put, 'She did her best' on my grave, but now you can put, 'She did even better.'" Mary Rose had been what she called "a dutiful wife," caring for house, husband and children and seldom doing anything for herself. That was, until she sat down that first day at table 12.

Robinson Leary, named after the famous baseball player, Jackie Robinson, had enjoyed a partnership relationship with her professor husband. They taught together, rode to the university every day together in their old Volvo, and loved reading, writing and good music. He had lived longer than many with multiple sclerosis and had been just as active in his wheelchair as any other professor in his department. Robbie didn't say anything at his grave; she just cried, kissed her flower, and started walking toward the mausoleum that housed the urn holding at least part of Hadley's husband.

That husband had loved Hadley with a passion, been proud of her and shown her off like some of his friends had paraded their new trophy wives. She was well-educated, independent and never once questioned that he was hers for life; a life that ended when that plane plowed into the Rocky Mountains and burned everything and everyone beyond recognition. She was pretty sure there were some airplane parts in the urn along with him, but it didn't matter. She knew his spirit was with her. She laid her flower in the niche holding the urn and said in a soft voice, "All is well, big guy. I'm still messing around with the sheriff."

On their trip west the year before, Hadley had met Wes Longbow, county sheriff and the most handsome Native American she had ever seen. They had enjoyed a gentle romance and talked about Wes coming to Omaha to start a private detective agency. He, like Hadley, was past retirement age and could do what he pleased, but he didn't like the city and Hadley wasn't willing to give up her friends and community. Wes did consulting with sheriffs' offices across the country, and he and Hadley met every other month for a week together.

The girls came out of the mausoleum and sat down in a small, comfortable garden furnished with a tasteful white cast iron table and four chairs.

Robbie sighed. "I read where people grieve in four ways: physically, emotionally, mentally and spiritually. I think I'm most mental. Maybe because I was a teacher, but after he died I read every book on grief I could find. I thought and wondered and for a long time couldn't keep my head clear no matter how simple the words."

Mary Rose nodded. "I was all physical. My heart and my head literally ached, I wanted to eat all the time, I was stiff and sore and on top of it all, I got the worst cold I'd had in years I ate all the time, then my stomach would hurt. I'm not even going to tell you what happened with my bowels!"

Hadley smiled at her. "I'm the emotional one, I guess. I cried almost constantly for a week or two. I read where one widow got a metal garbage can, went to the Goodwill store and bought a cheap set of dishes then smashed every one of them into the garbage can. I actually did that. I was so mad at him and the world I could have spit." She thought for a minute. "Actually, I did that, too." She looked at Calamity. "I guess that leaves you to tell us about how grief affected you spiritually, Calamity. Robbie has mental, Mary Rose has physical, and I just claimed emotional."

Calamity's face formed a little sneer. "Hah! Spiritual. I'll tell you my whole philosophy of spirituality. I learned it early in life through a story about a robin who decided to stay up north for the winter and not fly south. After a while though, it got cold with freezing rain, sleet and some snow. The rain froze his wing and he dropped down, down, down into a farmyard." She made a diving motion with one hand for the down, down, down.

"So he's there on the ground, ready to die from the cold when along comes a cow and craps on him. At first the robin thought he'd die for sure, but the crap was warm and the wing thawed and the robin revived and moved a little and was comfortable." She took a breath and continued. "But along came the farm cat. He saw the pile of crap moving, pounced on it, dug the robin out and ate him." She paused for emphasis. "The moral of this story, ladies, is my spirituality, dead husbands or not. *Everyone who craps on you is not necessarily your enemy.*

Everyone who rescues you from a pile of crap is not necessarily your friend.

And if you're comfortable living in a pile of crap, for Pete's sake, stay there."

Then Calamity stood up and started down the hill to their car. The other three stood and began to follow her, single file.

"Silly me," Mary Rose said, just loud enough for Robbie, walking just ahead of her to hear, "I thought she'd talk about prayer and meditation and how being in the circus taught her to never take life or love for granted. I thought maybe she'd say because death was so universal it must be a blessing."

"Silly, silly you," Robbie replied.

The Boys

One morning when soft thunder rolled across the plains and rain dripped down the big dining room windows, the girls, as they often did on stormy mornings, ended up in the fitness room at Meadow Lakes. Hadley and Robbie were doing three miles on the treadmills and watching Wolff Blitzer interview another suit on CNN. Mary Rose was puffing away on the Stairmaster and Calamity was flat on her back on the weight bench, smoothly lifting a bar with sixty pound weights on each end and not even breathing hard.

Suddenly Mrs. Goldberg huffed and puffed like the Big Bad Wolf into the room. She looked around. "Never been in here," she wheezed. "Not important.

I need to see the four of you right away." They stopped their exercise and moved toward the massive lady whose apron was wrongly proclaiming the day as Tuesday "I have a great favor to ask, and I just frosted a batch of nutty cinnamon rolls, thanks to Herman." She turned. They followed, trying to concentrate on Mrs. Goldberg's urgency and not on frosted rolls.

Mrs. Goldberg's apartment was crowded with oversized furniture. On the back of her big sofa, flat on top of a crotched afghan, lay Margaret Thatcher, her beady little cat eyes focused on a golden canary swinging in her cage and singing at the top of her tiny little lungs. Mrs. Goldberg pointed to the bird and said, "Princess Di. Caged for life and singing her precious little heart out, being watched every minute of the day." Margaret Thatcher's tail twitched back and forth, back and forth.

The delicious smell of cinnamon rolls coated the furniture, carpet and drapes. The savory odor was coming strongly from the little kitchen where a ceramic bowl sat, covered with a gingham cloth, in a warm spot near the oven. They hurried in.

Standing along the kitchen counter were four strange men. Robbie recognized the one on her right as Rueben, the Sasquatch cat chaser, who motioned them into chairs. Mrs. Goldberg oozed into the largest chair. The plate of cinnamon rolls sat in the middle of the table and four delicate china coffee cups waited in their saucers.

One of the men, dressed in a business suit, poured coffee for everyone. He turned toward them, took a little Bible out of his pocket, held it up and pointed it toward the cinnamon rolls. "Cinnamon rolls are bagels with sin attached. Please sin with us. Let us eat." It sounded as if he was quoting someone. Hadley, Mary Rose and Calamity looked toward Robbie, their literature and quotation expert. She shrugged. They each reached for a roll and a napkin from the holder on the table.

"My nephew Robert," Mrs. Goldberg said of the man who poured coffee and quoted. "He's a United Methodist minister, retired." She pointed to the cat chaser. "You haven't met him, but you've seen Rueben. He was in construction." Rueben nodded. The girls nodded and smiled but they couldn't help staring at the third man.

"This is Leonard," Mrs. Goldberg sighed. "He doesn't speak. He was abducted and probed by aliens and doesn't want them to find him. *If he stood beside Mrs. Goldberg, they could join the circus,* Calamity thought. Hadley blinked three times. Robbie bit her lip and Mary Rose leaned forward in her chair and willed her mouth to stay closed. Leonard was dressed in white pants, white shoes and socks and a white shirt buttoned to the top. His face was totally smooth and unlined. What they could see of his hair was also white as snow. The only color on his entire body was the silver aluminum foil three-cornered hat pressed down on his head. It was shaped like a pyramid and loomed

into the air a good sixteen inches above his head.
They were silent.

"It's a deflecting hat," Rueben said, pointing to the
weird headgear. "He believes that any alien beams
trying to track him will be deflected off the foil and
confuse the aliens."

Mary Rose opened her mouth and said, "Where was
he probed?"

"You don't want to know," Rueben said. Leonard
smiled demurely and shook his head.

"And this is sweet Clyde," Mrs. Goldberg said,
pointing to a seated gentleman dressed in a black
jogging suit with "Nebraska Blackshirts" across the
front. Clyde slid out of his chair and stood up, but
his height didn't change.

"You're a midget!" Mary Rose blurted out.

"Wrong!" the little man said, glaring at her. "I'm a
troll and don't you forget it. A tough, mean,
merciless troll. And don't call me a 'little person'
either. I object to that. Children are 'little people'.
Me, I'm definitely on the troll level."

Calamity and Robbie could see Clyde's feet on the floor by the edge of the table. He was wearing black women's wedgies with cork platforms and ankle straps tied in front.

"Cool shoes," Calamity said.

"Thanks." Clyde said, and he climbed back into his chair. Mrs. Goldberg smiled a sad smile at the four men. "My wonderful nephews. Different fathers." Everyone let the cinnamon rolls melt in their mouths and sipped their coffees.

Clyde the midget spoke up. "Aunt Evangeline's husband, our Uncle Eli, had a brother named Peyton," Clyde said, taking the storytelling lead. "Unfortunately, Peyton had an awful experience at his own funeral."

"That's hard to do," Calamity said.

Clyde rolled his eyes and ignored her. "We were at the funeral home. The funeral director had just wheeled Peyton's casket out to the foyer on its way into our viewing room. It was on that gurney thing when all hell broke loose in the viewing room in front of us, family name of Mazur. This skinny old broad from Trenton was complaining about it being a closed casket for her dearly departed and all at once she caught her sleeve or got her arm tangled up enough to tip the damn casket over. She lands on the floor along with the casket. It springs open, the candelabra starts weaving back and forth, the old lady yells, 'Terrible make-up.' and the curtains catch on fire."

"She was really a very nice lady," Mrs. Goldberg broke in. "I talked to her in the foyer. Her granddaughter brought her all the way from New Jersey just for the viewing."

"And her granddaughter was something else, too," Clyde continued. "She grabs Grandma, pulls her up and drags Granny's skinny ass outta there."

"But not before Grandma grabbed the entire plate of cookies and dumped them in her purse," Mrs. Goldberg added, with a little note of admiration.

"That's when the trouble starts," Clyde explained. "Digger O'Doul, the undertaker, grabs a fire extinguisher and right as he's running past the front door, it opens and in steps this goon with a gun.

"He shoots Digger square in the head!" Clyde's eyes were growing bigger. "Digger drops like a sack of cement."

Robert held up his Bible, "I say to you, that goon was hated by all the mothers in town for he was vulgar, lazy and bad!"

Robbie leaned toward Hadley. "That one was a take-off from Tom Sawyer," she whispered.

"And Digger was a very friendly undertaker," Mrs. Goldberg added.

Clyde took a breath, "The friggin' place is on fire, the gun goon sees Grandma making tracks and heads into the room with the fire instead of coming after us, his targets in the first place. So the boys and I grab the gurney and *we* make tracks and get the casket and Peyton out the back door. We load it into the hearse and hightail it to the cemetery."

"You stole a hearse?" Robbie asked.

"Had to. You can't get a casket in Rueben's van. It has seats and all. Anyways, a hearse looks natural going to the cemetery."

"We had a real proper burial," Mrs. Goldberg said, wiping a tear from her eye.

Clyde scowled. "I'll say it like it is. Peyton had some mob connections. He was a gambler and did some shady stuff that led to a rather large need to steal our mother's very nice, very expensive necklace." Clyde's voice was rising. He was turning into an angry little troll.

"And there were complications," Rueben added.

"Kinda," Clyde said. "The mob sent the gun goon to get the necklace. See, Peyton knew he didn't have long to live because he'd crossed the mob more than once." Clyde paused.

"Or twice," Rueben injected.

"Let me count the ways," Robert said, holding his Bible.

Leonard held up both hands to show all ten fingers.

The girls were turning their heads from speaker to speaker; eyes wide, mouths open just a little.

Clyde took control again. "See, Peyton wanted to go out with the necklace instead of turning it over to the mob. He made funeral pre-arrangements so he could take it with him. Went to Digger, picked out his casket and slipped the necklace into one of those cute little drawers some caskets have to hold mementos and stuff."

"Then the poor dear died," Mrs. Goldberg said. "Mysteriously," Leonard hung his head and nodded.

"If you can call two broken legs and a smashed-in back of the head mysterious," Clyde sneered.

"We took him to the cemetery right then and there, way before the police arrived," Mrs. Goldberg said.

"We buried him all by ourselves. The boys dug the grave." She smiled at her nephews. "Lucky for us there was a backhoe by the edge of the cemetery and Leonard can hot-wire anything."

Mrs. Goldberg looked to the ceiling as if remembering every detail. "The boys dropped, well...*lowered,* the casket into the ground."

"It wasn't a real expensive casket," Clyde added.

"Robert said a few words," Mrs. Goldberg said, smiling at Robert, who smiled a tender smile back.

"Robert said *a LOT* of words," Rueben said. "Way too many words. Not needed words."

"It was a sacred moment!" Robert almost yelled.

"It was more like a sacred *hour!*" Rueben yelled.

"We finally had to shut him up," Clyde said softly.

"Rueben glared at Clyde. "And I *could* have got the damn casket in the van if you'd helped, you little squirt."

"Don't call me a squirt, Bigfoot!" Clyde yelled.

"A soft word turneth away wrath," Robert yelled, and he pointed his Bible at Clyde then Rueben. Leonard hopped up and sat on the kitchen counter as far away as possible and began swinging his legs.

Mrs. Goldberg hoisted herself out of her chair in one lunge, looked at the girls and pointed to the living room. They followed, loud voices surrounding them as they hurried from the kitchen.

In the living room, Princess Di had stopped singing. She and Margaret Thatcher were watching the action in the kitchen.

"I'm sorry about that," Mrs. Goldberg said. The four friends gave her sympathetic looks. "It's because of all those different fathers. That's why I need you girls. They can't do something this big and this important alone. They need grounding. They need supervision; a woman's touch and I'm too big and old to traipse around after them."

They had settled into the big, overly soft sofa and chairs in the cramped living room.. There was a short silence then angrier words drifted toward them from the nephews.

"Idiot!"

"Moron!"

"Heathen!"

"My van!"

Robbie broke the silence. "Just what is it you need us to do, Mrs. Goldberg?"

"Why to help the boys open poor Peyton's grave and retrieve the necklace from the buried casket, of course," Mrs. Goldberg said.

"You've got to be kidding!" Hadley said.

"No way would we do that!" Robbie frowned.

"That could be exciting," Mary Rose added hopefully. They looked at her.

"I've dug up a body and robbed a grave," Calamity announced, looking at Mary Rose. "She's right. It can be *real* exciting." She almost smiled again.

"That is definitely illegal," Hadley said. "I know. My son's a lawyer."

"It's not so terribly illegal or wrong," Mrs. Goldberg said. "And that necklace rightfully belongs to the boys." The boys were still at it in the kitchen.

"Dupe!"

"Ignoramus!"

"Den of vipers!"

Bang!

Apparently Leonard had kicked the cupboard to get his two cents in.

"Actually," Mrs. Goldberg smiled. "Poor Peyton is buried in a family cemetery."

"That's a relief," Hadley said, looking at Robbie.

"But if it's your family cemetery, you can have it legally exhumed easily I should think," Robbie said. "You wouldn't need us for that,"

Calamity raised her eyebrows, cocked her head and looked at Mrs. Goldberg. The yelling from the kitchen had stopped and voices turned to a conspiratorial murmur.

"There is one little problem," Mrs. Goldberg said. "This family cemetery where the body is buried? It doesn't belong to *our* family." There was a pause. Margaret Thatcher turned toward Princess Di who turned toward her food cup. They waited. Mrs. Goldberg shrugged a massive shrug. "Rueben was driving the hearse," she explained. "He has a terrible sense of direction and the cemeteries were very close to each other. He missed ours by about a quarter mile." The girls stared at her. No one could think of anything to say.

Clyde led the parade out of the kitchen. He was grinning. Rueben followed him, so tall that Clyde's head was just above his silver belt bucket. Robert had pocketed the Bible and Leonard was trailing along, glancing behind as if he were being followed.

"We made a decision," Clyde said, grin widening. "We figured if all of us are working together we're a team. So if you're The BOOB Girls. . ." He spread his little arms out toward his strange-looking brothers. "Ladies, meet the BOOB Boys." Before he could finish, Rueben broke in. "The Burned Out Old Bastards."

Grave Robbing for Dummies

They were all gathered in one of the Conversation Rooms on the second floor of Meadow Lakes Retirement Community. Robert had pulled two round tables together for what looked like any almost normal business conference. Two pots of coffee, regular and decaf, had been provided by the Meadow Lakes staff and of course, Mrs. Goldberg had provided the cinnamon rolls. Calamity and Clyde had taken the lead in the brainstorming session on how to get the necklace from the grave.

Clyde was wearing jeans, a Go Big Red long-sleeved t-shirt in a small men's size and tasteful red wedgies with black trim. In an interesting and somewhat frightening coincidence, Calamity was wearing jeans, a Go Big Red long-sleeved t-shirt in a woman's size small and black sneakers. She was leaning across the table toward him. "So who owns the cemetery where you buried Peyton?"

"The Bear family," Clyde answered.

"I don't mean, do they have animals," Calamity said patiently, "who are they?"

"The Bear family," Clyde said with equal patience. "Their name is 'Bear,' the Solomon Bear family. They were our neighbors when we lived in the country. Solomon came to Iowa in 1850. He was a big old bearded dude according to his pictures. The cemetery is in the middle of where an old orchard stood. Kinda rough getting to it, too."

Hadley leaned toward Robbie, "We cross state lines in this fiasco? Cross the river into Iowa?"

70

"So, who owns the land now?" Calamity persisted.

"Big dude named Ted. Folks call him Teddy."

"Teddy Bear? "Now I know you're kidding!"
Hadley said, shaking her head.

"Teddy Bear. That is so cute," Mary Rose said,
reaching over and touching Mrs. Goldberg's arm.
Mrs. Goldberg smiled and nodded.

"No one is named Teddy Bear," Robbie said.
"It's true," Rueben said,
Leonard nodded vigorously.
"I'm so sorry we made a wrong turn and went into
the Bear cemetery," Mrs. Goldberg said. "We
failed poor Peyton." Her voice sounded pitiful.

Robert pulled out his Bible and took a deep breath.
"Therefore, after every failure, we are obliged to
strive again for success, and when faced with the
end of one thing, we must build something new and
better in the ashes, just as from pain and grief, we
must weave hope." He pocketed the Bible, moved
behind his aunt and began rubbing her shoulders.

71

"I know that one!" Robbie said excitedly. "That's Dean Koontz." She pointed a finger at Robert and smiled. He pointed a finger back and winked.

"It sounds as if the Bears were good neighbors," Hadley said. "Why can't you just tell them the truth and let them help you?"

"Problem is," Rueben said, "they don't live on the home place anymore. They went to Orlando and have good jobs at Disney World. Can't find 'em."

"It's really pretty simple," Calamity said, looking at Clyde. "We do this at dusk so we can see our way in, get the grave open and the necklace secured then make our way out after dark. No one's going to be watching us are they?" She looked at each one of the BOOB Boys and then at Mrs. Goldberg.

Robbie and Hadley were frowning. Mary Rose's eyes were wide and she was smiling

"We don't think the mob knows where the body is or even if the necklace is in the casket," Rueben said. "We think the gun goon was just going to look in the casket and search Peyton's body. That little drawer is like a secret compartment."

"YOU think that, you big idiot!" Clyde said loudly. "Of course we'll be watched. The mob can put two and two together. They probably know the truth about where the necklace is."

Robert, still standing behind Mrs. Goldberg, pulled out his Bible once again. "Only enemies speak the truth," he said, waving the book back and forth, "friends and lovers are endlessly caught up in the line of duty."

Robbie, caught up in the whole thing, stood up. "Stephen King!" she yelled.

"Bingo!" Robert yelled back.

"Oh, for Pete's sake," Hadley said.

Mary Rose was grinning from ear to ear and Calamity was almost smiling again. Mrs. Goldberg smiled, sighed and shook her head.

"I think we need one reliable man in on this," Hadley said, standing up and giving up any idea of preventing an actual grave robbing. She was looking down the table toward Calamity, raising her voice even louder than the brothers'.

The little spy nodded. "Go get him, Hadley."

In just a few minutes, while the boys were still yelling at each other and the girls and Mrs. Goldberg were watching with quiet wisdom, the door opened and Hadley stepped inside.

"Come on in Wiley," she said. "We're planning to rob a grave."

T'was A Dark and Stormy Night

Calamity had told them all to wear black, so on that early evening, under a threatening cloud cover that stretched as far as the eye could see, nine strange figures slipped out one of the back doors of Meadow Lakes Retirement Community and moved toward an ancient van parked at the end of the short sidewalk. Wiley Vondra, sporting a black Stetson and dressed in black jeans, black cowboy shirt, black boots and wearing his brown vest, broke off from the other eight and headed for the garages, where he would get in his small black pickup truck and follow them to the cemetery.

Mrs. Goldberg, her massive frame filling the glass door they had just exited, waved a handkerchief she had retrieved from the pocket of her Friday apron. Just before they closed the door she handed Mary Rose a basket of cinnamon rolls covered with a black cloth.

"Oh my God, Rueben!" Robbie said as she opened the door to the van. "This is a mess!"

Hadley looked inside. "Rueben, this is a landfill." She put her hand over her nose.

"I always thought it looked more like it belonged to a deranged social worker," Clyde said.

Mary Rose looked inside. "Does anyone have any handy-wipes?"

75

Robert put his hand in his pocket to pull out his Bible, looked inside the van, shook his head and simply patted the book.

Calamity and Rueben said nothing; they just climbed into the front seats.

All the boys except Leonard had black hats or caps hiding their white or grey hair. Since none of the women had black hats or scarves, Calamity had given them each a black umbrella, which she called stakeout souvenirs. The umbrellas would hide their hair while they walked to the grave. All the girls wore black jackets. Snuggled into the right hand pocket of each of their jackets were the little angels given to them by Calamity. Calamity's angel was in her left jacket pocket. She had a small revolver in the right.

Calamity was in her black body suit and had a ski mask rolled up on her forehead. Her shoes looked as if they had cleats attached, and she threw her big black bag onto the floor before she climbed in.

The van had three rows of seats. Mary Rose pulled herself in and headed for the back. As she sat down, the seat sank nearly to the floor. "Yikes!" she said loudly, "these springs are broke." She clutched the basket of cinnamon rolls tighter. Robert climbed in after her, brushing newspapers and food wrappers off the seat. The seat sank lower. As Robbie climbed in, a wrapper from some long-discarded fast food delight stuck to the sole of her shoe. She looked back at Hadley, lifted her foot, and Hadley pulled the wrapper off, wadded it up and stuck it in her jacket pocket. Then she grabbed the hand grip and pulled herself up, taking a seat in the second row. The springs held.

Next in was Leonard. He had refused to wear anything other than his usual all white, so he was decked out in a long black raincoat that came to his ankles and covered the white. Hadley thought it probably belonged to his aunt Evangeline because it could easily have reached around him twice. His shoes, however, were bright white as was his hair that stuck out from under the aluminum foil hat.

"He looks like disembodied head and feet," Robbie whispered to Hadley.

"Maybe he'll blend in with other cemetery ghosts," Hadley whispered back.

No one had helped Clyde into the van. He stood outside the wide door, hands on his hips. "Okay smartasses. How do I get in?"

To their surprise, it was Calamity who opened her passenger-side door, jumped out, hurried around the front of the van and with no effort whatsoever, hoisted Clyde inside.

"I wish I could do that," Mary Rose said.

"Don't we all?" Robert added.

Looking out the dirty window, Hadley saw Wiley's pickup pull out of his garage and roll quietly around to the wide driveway in front of Meadow Lakes. Wiley would wait a few minutes after the van passed him, then follow at a distance to make sure the mob wasn't joining the party and tailing them.

Rueben turned the key in the van's ignition. A low, rumbling Rrrrrrr sounded but nothing happened. He tried again, leaning forward over the steering wheel as if that would help. Robbie and Hadley turned and looked at Mary Rose and Robert who looked back and shrugged at the same time. After the fourth try, Rueben turned and looked at Leonard. Leonard slid the door open, jumped out, scampered to the front of the van and lifted the hood. In less than a minute the engine started and Leonard pulled himself inside, his coat trailing behind him like Batman's cape. He slammed the sliding door shut but not the entire coat made it inside. As they pulled out of the Meadow Lakes parking lot, nearly a yard of black fabric was flapping merrily along against the side of the rusty van.

A Cemetery of Bears

Plan A was for Wiley to follow them to make sure they were alone. There was no Plan B. They passed his pickup, parked under the canopy in the circle drive by the front entrance. As they pulled out, Mary Rose gave him a little finger wave.

The ride in the van was uncomfortable to say the least. The springs had given up long ago, it tended to lean to one side and it felt as if the tires were square. There was an unidentifiable smell that permeated the entire interior and seemed to be a combination of decayed French fries and stale smoke. Whether the smoke smell came from cigars, cigarettes or the van itself was anybody's guess.

As they passed the Old Market and headed toward the I-80 Bridge that spanned the Missouri River and would take them into Iowa, Calamity's cell phone vibrated. She flipped it open.

"Yo," she said, listened then clicked it off.

"Wiley's three blocks back. We're in the clear."

They were bounced around mercilessly. "Just imagine this is a carnival ride," Hadley said.

"Suffering is optional," Robbie said. "How we handle this says a lot about who we are."

80

"So does lost luggage," Robbie continued. Hadley looked at her. "You can tell a lot about a person by how she handles lost luggage." Hadley shook her head and did an eye roll.

"Or tangled Christmas tree lights," Mary Rose added.

"Or having a Milk Dud box put down your pants, or your wedgies painted purple, or your fingers super glued to your crotch while you sleep, or…" Clyde's voice was steadily rising.

"Cool it, Clyde!" Calamity said.

Clyde cooled it and Hadley reached over and patted his shoulder.

Wiley was far enough behind them that they couldn't see the lights from his pickup. He had put the location of the cemetery into his GPS and Rueben had assured him it was accurate. Still, it was a worry for Mary Rose. She tried glancing out the back windows, but that was a useless effort. Hadley kept looking at her watch and sighing. Each time she sighed, Clyde sighed.

As they turned onto a side road just past the lights of Council Buffs, the van backfired. They all, with the exception of Leonard, let out a gasp and squeal. Clyde's came out as a squeak, then they laughed nervously.

After fifteen minutes of silence, they were in hilly country near the beautiful Loess Hills that bordered Council Bluffs. More than one hundred years before Lewis and Clark would stay in these hills in White Catfish Camp, French and Spanish traders had settled in to what today is Long's Landing. Lakota Indians had occupied the hills and held council there and Omaha (which means Going Against the Wind) was named after one of these Lakota tribes. Even now, after heavy rains, arrowheads can be found in the red clay and rich soil. In just a few minutes, Rueben stopped the van.

Ahead of them was a neat, fairly new sign that read, "Bear Cemetery."

"And you missed that sign and turned in here by mistake, you idiot," Clyde said. Calamity put her hand on his shoulder.

"Cool it again, Clyde," Calamity said in a low, growling voice. Clyde cooled it again.

If the ride to the turnoff was bumpy, it was a trip on velvet compared to the rutted path up hill to the cemetery. They bounced, jarred and rolled over bumps, tree roots and small logs. More than once tree branches scraped the van, sounding like an attack of screeching birds with an attitude. At one point, after they dipped into a particularly deep rut, the van protested so much Hadley and Robbie offered to get out and walk.

Rueben pulled the van to a stop in front of what looked like a virtual forest in the rapidly growing dusk. Then he eased it underneath a huge maple tree with branches so thick the van was completely hidden in its darkness. He looked at Leonard.

83

"Think the Jesus Van will start again if I turn her off?" Leonard nodded.

"Jesus Van?" Mary Rose asked from the back where she was still clutching the basket of rolls so tight her knuckles were white.

"After Chip Davis' song, *Convoy,*" Rueben said, "You know," and he began to sing in a soft baritone. "Eleven long-haired friends of Jesus in a chartreuse mini-van." Robert and Clyde joined him in the last word, "Convoooy…"

"Crap!" Calamity said. Robbie, Hadley, Mary Rose and Leonard all smiled.

And the Raven, Never Flitting, Still is Sitting, Still is Sitting

The climb out of the van was as slow and laborious as the climb in. The step to the ground was high, so they all grabbed the hand hold and backed out. By the time Leonard jumped out, black coat flapping happily, Calamity and Rueben were unloading the shovels, umbrellas and bags from the back. Calamity's big bag was slung over her shoulder and balanced on her back. Robert helped Clyde, who jumped out awkwardly. They walked behind the van to gather their gear and whatever else needed to be carried to the grave. Only Mary Rose stayed where she was, looking back down the dark, rutted path. "I don't see Wiley yet," she said. No one heard her, and no one knew that the vehicle approaching the "Bear Cemetery" sign was not Wiley Vondra's black pickup truck, but a sleek gray Suburban with an ominous looking logo on the side.

"Open 'em up and hold 'em close," Calamity said, handing the umbrellas to the three other women. "If there's anybody in the woods, they may see Leonard's head and shoes, but they won't see you, and if they can't see you they can't shoot you." They opened 'em up and held 'em close. They started up the hill, Leonard's hair, hat and feet seemingly floating along without a body.

"Spooky," Robbie said. An acorn fell from a tree and bounced off her umbrella.

"Strange and eerie," Hadley said, ducking under a branch.

"Exciting," Mary Rose said. "I feel just like Nancy Drew."

"A seasoned, thickened Nancy Drew," Hadley observed.

"Nancy Drew would have had exclamation points," Robbie said. "She had more exclamation points than anyone."

"We could have exclamation points!" Hadley said, a little too loud.

"We deserve exclamation points!" Robbie said a little louder.

"Exclamation points are us!" Mary Rose finished.

"Quiet!" Calamity hissed. They were quiet. Her exclamation points had muscle!

They made their way through trees and over rough ground. Soon all three umbrellas were folded and being used as walking sticks. From somewhere on their right a small animal scurried away, leaves crackling. An owl hooted and black wings flapped overhead.

"I feel as if I'm walking into Edgar Allen Poe country," Robbie said, looking after the big bird as it flew into the trees. When she turned back, a branch hit her in the face. "Ow!"

Rueben and Calamity were leading the way with Leonard and Robert close behind. Clyde was scurrying along at Robert's heels, dragging a big tube bag behind him. Every so often, his wedgies caused him to twist an ankle and he mumbled a soft cuss word.

"It would be nice if one of those gentlemen was polite enough to walk back here with us and help us over some of this crap," Mary Rose growled.

"Hey, Girl," Hadley said. "Who needs them?" She turned forward, tripped over a tree root and fell flat.

"Ow!" Robbie and Mary Rose grabbed her hands and helped her up. The umbrella she was holding lay behind as they moved on.

"Look," Robbie whispered, waiting for the other two to catch up with her. She was pointing into the woods where the fading light showed two huge brown eyes staring at them. "It's a deer." As soon as they moved, the deer bounded away. From somewhere in the distance a coyote howled.

"Coyotes? Here?" Mary Rose said.

"They were around my grandmother's farm in Iowa," Hadley whispered.

"There are reports of mountain lions around these hills, too," Robbie whispered.

Just then a flash of lightning lit up the western sky, a clap of thunder sounded and darkness fell. Overhead, a large crow settled into a giant pine tree.

At the crest of the hill was a beautiful old wrought iron fence and gate with the words, "Bear Family," in the middle of a black iron wagon wheel.

An ancient backhoe was just inside the gate along with some unidentified tools and boxes. Ahead of them, Calamity was peering into an open grave. Rueben was beside her, holding a large flashlight, its beam pointing down into the grave. Beside him, Robert was holding onto Clyde who was leaning so far over the grave it looked as if he could go in head first any minute. Clyde was still holding onto the long, narrow tube that was nearly as tall as he was. Leonard was at the head of the grave, arms folded, looking proud and still bodiless.

"He came out at dawn, hotwired the back hoe and did this all by himself," Clyde said as Hadley, Mary Rose and Robbie arrived beside him.

Leonard's work was impressive. The grave was not only open, but there was also a space of at least two feet surrounding the brown casket, its metal reflecting in the flashlight beam. The big box rested well over six feet below the ground. A huge mound of dirt was piled at the foot of the grave. Leonard had done a thorough job with the back hoe and shovels would only be needed to close the grave. The three girls made their way carefully to the edge of the black hole.

"My God," Hadley said, leaning over and looking into the grave. "We could all stand in there, hold hands and sing 'Kumbaya.'"

"Sweet Jesus," Robbie added, looking down into the grave.

"Holy Mother of God," Mary Rose said softly.

"They already had the religious service, ladies," Calamity said. "Let's get on with it." She opened her black bag, pulled out a narrow coil of rope and began tying it around a small tree. When she was finished, she grabbed hold of the rope and easily lowered herself into the grave. The top of her head was well below the ground.

"Looks easy," Hadley said, looking down into the damp hole. "I've never been in a grave before," and she grabbed the rope, turned her back to the casket, put one foot on the steep side of the grave and fell with a loud bang onto the casket. "Ow!" she said.

"That's going to make a bruise," Mary Rose said. Robbie nodded, grabbed the rope and went down, very carefully.

Rueben had simply jumped into the grave, Clyde stood on one side, standing guard and messing with the long tube that had never left his hands. Leonard stood at the head of the grave. Robert stayed on the other side next to Mary Rose. She looked up at him. "I'm going down, Robert," she said with a dramatic flair and handed him the basket of rolls. "I love adventure." Robert nodded and set the basket on the ground. There was no sign of Wiley Vondra, but the woods behind them had fallen silent. The few tombstones left in the old cemetery were silent too, as if they were watching and waiting.

"It's really rather cozy down here," Robbie said. Hadley did an eye roll. The ground smelled of spring promises and new things ready to grow.

All four women and Rueben were in the grave. "It's right here," Rueben said, moving next to Calamity and pointing to the end of the casket where the feet would be. Calamity felt around for a tiny spring to open the memento drawer. Families frequently wrote notes to the deceased, children drew pictures and sometimes photos were put in these little drawers and buried with a loved one.

"Found the drawer. Thing is locked." Calamity reached into the belt she had strapped around her waist. The instrument she pulled out looked something like a dentist's pick. Rueben continued to hold the light steady. After just a few seconds there was a tiny click and the drawer sprang open. Calamity reached inside.

"Borsheim box!" she exclaimed. Borsheim's is the largest jewelry store in the country and owned by Omahan Warren Buffett.

There was a communal breath-holding as Calamity slowly opened the box. Even in the dark, they could see the sparkle of the diamonds in the light

92

from Rueben's flashlight. It was beautiful; a fairytale necklace of diamonds and rubies that had to cost into six figures. Calamity closed the box almost reverently and handed it to Rueben, who stuck it securely into his jacket pocket.

Just as Rueben turned toward the rope to climb out of the grave there was the pounding sound of running feet and a terrifying scream from the direction of the path they had followed. A small figure in a black Ninja body suit, black shoes and a hooded shirt ran at break-neck speed toward the grave, screaming all the way. Lightning flashed again and reflected off the gun held in his hand. He screamed again and dived into the grave, pointing the gun with fatal accuracy at Calamity's head.

"Well, Henry," Calamity said with eerie calmness, looking not at the gun but at the man holding it.

The loud sound of a gunshot came, not from inside the grave but from above. Clyde had pulled a gun almost as big as he was out of his long tube. They all watched in fear and amazement as the kick from the rifle lifted the little man into the air and threw him with terrific force against a tree.

"Ow!" he yelled.

"Lots of kick there," Rueben said.

"Robert!" Hadley yelled. They looked up to see Robert grab his chest and fall to the ground, hit by the blast from Clyde's gun. The wiry, Ninja-like man in the grave couldn't help but look up and when he did, Calamity flew into the air and sent her feet flying into his head. As the force of the kick knocked her away, there was a second shot from above the grave. The Ninja fell forward over the casket and Hadley saw a pair of handcuffs fly into the grave and into Calamity's hands. Calamity grabbed the Ninja's arms, pulled them behind him and snapped the cuffs onto his wrists.

Hadley looked up. Standing directly over her, in cowboy boots and white cowboy hat was the most handsome Indian she had ever seen. "Hey, Wes," she said and she smiled a nervous smile, dirt streaked on her cheek.

"Hi Honey, I'm home," Wes Longbow said. The sheriff had arrived.

Wiley Vondra was squatted down, bending over Robert who was sitting up and reaching into his pocket.

Rueben was pulling Robbie out of the grave with one hand and reaching the other toward Mary Rose. Hadley had grabbed Wes' hand and was climbing out as well. Calamity was climbing up the rope, making it look disgustingly easy. Robbie was watching Robert work his Bible carefully out of his pocket. "He's not going to hold that book up and quote something now, is he?" she said.

"I don't think so," Wiley answered, looking back at them and grinning. Robert did hold up the Bible, but not to deliver a quote. As another lightning bolt lit the sky they could see a hole in the thick little book. Clyde's bullet had hit Holy ground.

Clyde was wobbling toward Robert, crying openly. He dived into his brother's arms and they both fell backward onto the ground. A light rain began to fall. Hadley was talking to Wes, motioning toward the grave then pointing to each of the BOOB boys. Wes was nodding and following her gestures. Rueben was dragging the unconscious Ninja out of the hole. Calamity had her watch open calling for a clean-up. Robbie and Mary Rose were standing beside Leonard, watching the whole thing.

They walked down the path in a gentle rain. A black Hummer was waiting beside the van. The same three men who had hurried into Calamity's apartment and removed unconscious husband number five met them and shoved Henry the Ninja, husband number six, moaning and groaning, into the back of the Hummer. Calamity climbed in with the three men in black, and the big vehicle backed up and rolled silently toward the road.

Rueben had stayed behind with Leonard to help fill the grave and finish with shovels what the backhoe couldn't do. Robert, shaken and a little light headed, was standing by Wes Longbow's silver Suburban, leaning on Mary Rose.

Wes opened the doors, one of which bore a black and gold logo saying, "Longbow Consulting" in a circle over a picture of a gun and a badge. On the bottom were the words, "Call the Sheriff." Hadley slipped into the passenger seat. Clyde pulled himself in and took a back seat along with Robbie and Mary Rose. Wiley held Robert's elbow and helped him in, then climbed in behind him. They were dirty, tired and almost as shaken as Robert.

"I saw Wes pull up just as I circled 'round front to wait for you," Wiley said. "I didn't tell him what you all were doing. I just parked my truck, jumped into his Suburban and told him he didn't want to miss this."

"I'm glad you didn't!" Hadley said, patting Wes' knee. She looked around. "We need wind down time. I want to go to Happy Hollow Country Club and have a good glass of wine." Wes, who was not tired, dirty or shaken, smiled. "Sounds like a plan."

"We aren't dressed for a country club," Clyde said from the back.

"Hey," Hadley said. "I've got friends in high places. My buddy Kelly will hide us in the Library with the best server in the place."

"I love that Arnold Palmer drink. Do they make Arnold Palmers there?" Clyde asked Robbie.

"Honey, it's a golf course," she said, smiling and leaning toward him.

"I'm going to buy a vineyard and grow a new wine," Mary Rose announced. "You know how they have Pinot Grigio and Pinot Noir? Well this wine is going to be an anti-diuretic so seniors can drink it at night and not have to get up and go to the bathroom." She grinned and looked around. "I'm calling it Pinot More." Wes laughed and turned on the windshield wipers.

Back at the cemetery, Rueben and Leonard were finishing up their grave work in a gentle rain while three raccoons were finishing off some really delicious cinnamon rolls and a very large crow was gathering up the crumbs. Two black umbrellas lay abandoned by the gate.

Part Three

How to be A One-Breasted Amazon

*I've never in my life worn a pink ribbon
and I don't plan to start now.*
Mary Rose

*Friends can help you cry and never mind it.
If they mind it, they're not your friend.*
Hadley Joy

*Illness instructs us.
Pain informs us.
Sorrow develops our soul.*
Robert (his own quote)

*Life is a sexually transmitted condition
that is one-hundred percent fatal.*
Robbie

*Women over 50 are dignified. They seldom have a
screaming match with you at the opera or in the
middle of an expensive restaurant. Of course, if you
deserve it, they won't hesitate to shoot you if they
think they can get away with it.* Andy Rooney

Days for the BOOB Girls and the BOOB Boys had returned to normal with just a small amount of welcome spring boredom. Fourteen varieties of Iris plants colored the back lawn at Meadow Lakes. The weather was beautiful, filled with the scent of flowering trees. Blossoms fell from crabapples, turning the ground into a pink carpet.

Mrs. Goldberg and her nephews had their necklace. Everyone buried in the Bear Cemetery was resting in peace. The boys were spending time in the pool room arguing and trying to master the game. Mrs. Goldberg, Margaret Thatcher and Princess Di were reveling in the sweet smell of cinnamon rolls in their apartment. Hadley and Wes had taken a short trip to the Amana Colonies in eastern Iowa before Wes drove on to his next consulting job. Wiley had returned to his card games and Mary Rose had returned from a brief visit with one of her daughters. She was happy and relieved to get home. No one had seen Calamity.

Robbie had stayed at Meadow Lakes and relaxed. She paid a visit to Peyton Claireborne, their hair stylist, and treated herself to a spa treatment at his Old Market salon. She spent considerable time at a local bookstore called The Bookworm, she drank coffee in The Village Grinder next door and had devoured at least five new mystery novels.

Now she was standing in the Meadow Lakes library, ready to donate an armload of books for other residents. The library had the usual big windows, a fireplace, tasteful floor lamps and tables covered with magazines. Two walls were floor-to-ceiling book shelves and there was a small desk for the volunteer librarian, Loretta Ripp. Loretta was, as Robbie described her, "a lovable flake."

"She's one bra hook short of a full lift," Hadley had observed after they had spent a morning cozied up with magazines and coffee.

"She's one banana short of a fruit salad," Robbie had offered.

"I like her, though," Mary Rose had said, and they all agreed.

Today, Loretta Ripp was excited. She was wearing a red skirt, white sneakers with anklets, a white, long-sleeved blouse and a bright green vest. She looked a little like a female spirit of Christmas just past and a bit worn. Her glasses had brown rims and because she thought librarians always had a pencil stuck behind their ears, she had a pencil stuck behind her ear.

"Robinson," she said, taking the books from Robbie's arms. "Guess what? I had a call from Kathleen, the head of the Omaha Area Library Association?" She took a deep breath. "Remember *Calendar Girls*? Older ladies with no clothes on but nice things held in front of their personal parts?" Loretta ended nearly every sentence with a question mark and a slight Minnesota accent.

Robbie nodded. "Good movie and a very tasteful calendar."

"Well, Kathleen is going to create a calendar as a fundraiser for area libraries and even though I'm just a volunteer, I get to be in it? It's called *Naked Librarians!*" Loretta was so excited she actually gave a little jump with a squeak and a giggle. "We'll all be holding books over our personal parts and I've chosen my two favorites books?" She giggled.

"Oh my gosh, Loretta. What books did you choose?"

"*Splendors of the Past* and *After the Fall*," Loretta said, picking up two books from her desk and holding one over each breast.

Robbie smiled. "Perfect for you." She avoided looking at Loretta's fallen chest.

As Robbie left the library, she nearly collided with a smiling, rested Calamity Doodles.

"Calamity! I was worried. How are you? Where have you been?"

If Men had to get Penisgrams

"Like old times," Hadley said as they sat down for breakfast. The morning was bright and there was happy chatter from the other diners surrounding them. The three at the table were all in lightweight jogging suits, ready for a walk through the cemetery after breakfast. Mary Rose was just coming through the big doors leading from her wing.

"She looks awfully serious for such a nice day," Hadley said.

"Hey, she's been visiting her kids. It takes some time to recover," Calamity said.

"Okay, what's up Mary Rose?" Robbie asked as Mary Rose pulled out her chair.

Mary Rose sat down with a thud. "I found a lump," she said softly.

"Oh crap," Calamity said and she looked away.

"Listen," Robbie said, reaching over and taking hold of Mary Rose's arm. "I've had lumps on lumps and they were all cysts. No sweat."

"I know," Mary Rose said. "I googled 'Breast Lump' and 'Breast Cancer' right after I found it. One site said eighty percent of lumps are benign."

Hadley didn't say anything. When she had her biopsy for uterine cancer her cute doc had assured her that only *five* percent of uterine bleeds at her age were cancer. She had been in that lousy five percent. Her surgery had been years ago and she was still anxious before her annual checkup.

"I'll have to get a mammogram," Mary Rose said, 'and I absolutely hate those."

"Me, too," Robbie said.

"If men had to have penisgrams they'd invent a better way," Calamity sneered.

Mary Rose shivered. "It's been at least three years for me." She looked at Hadley. "I know I'm

106

chicken about it, but I hate that squeeze and I hate waiting for the results. I'm scared."

"I know," Hadley agreed. She sat up straighter and brightened. "I know. Let's all go together and get them. There's that new cancer center that gives results right after the reading. We could turn it into an anxiety party. Misery loves company. A shared fear is a fear diminished and all that good stuff."

Robbie smiled at her. "You sound like Robert."

Hadley looked at her and pointed a well-manicured finger in Robbie's direction. "So when did you have your last one, Professor?"

Robbie smiled and added in her head. "Eighteen months ago."

"You're due." She pointed to Calamity.

Calamity added in her head. "Twenty eight years ago," she said.

"You're kidding!" Robbie and Hadley said together. Mary Rose's eyes got big and she leaned forward.

"So? Look at me. I don't *have* breasts. I have nipples on hot pads. There's nothing there to squeeze, and the only time I had one it hurt so bad I instinctively kicked the nurse."

Hadley smiled a wicked little smile. "Mine was two years ago, so we're all ready for a girlfriend thing."

"I'd like that," Mary Rose said. She actually smiled and looked relieved. "Come on, Calamity. The machines they have now are much better than what they had at first."

Hadley pulled out her phone, tapped the screen for her browser and googled the cancer center. When she told the receptionist about Mary Rose's lump, she made appointments for the day after tomorrow, just before lunch.

"Perfect," Hadley said. "We can celebrate good news with lunch in the Old Market." Robbie nodded and grinned, Calamity moaned and grumbled and Mary Rose said, "Thanks, Girls."

They did all they could to distract Mary Rose while they waited for their appointment. They walked, they played cards with Wiley, they beat Robert, Rueben and Leonard at pool, even though only Calamity had ever played, but Clyde creamed them every game. They had a cinnamon rolls and flavored coffee picnic on the patio with Mrs. Goldberg. Mary Rose said she couldn't sleep for worrying even though she was sure everything was all right. In fact, none of them slept all that well those two nights. Late afternoon the day before they were to go to the cancer center, Mary Rose announced that she wanted to visit her husband's grave - alone.

They watched as she drove away.

"I'm worried," Hadley said.

"I'm scared," Robbie said.

Calamity didn't say anything. She just watched Mary Rose's old Chrysler Concorde lumber out of the Meadow Lakes driveway and head toward the cemetery.

A Dangerous Profession

The waiting area of what Calamity called, "the chamber of horrors" was very modern, very pleasant and very comfortable. A coffee bar with protein snacks and coffee and teas stood against one wall. Soft, relaxing music played. Spread out on tables around the room was more information about breasts than anyone could ever use.

There were only two women ahead of them, but even so, they all kept glancing at their watches. At exactly the time of their appointment, a young, pretty nurse with a nametag reading, "Jessi," came out of a door leading into the mammogram room. She glanced at her clipboard, looked at them and said, "Mary Rose, Robinson, Calamity," her eyebrows lifted just a little when she read Calamity's name, "and Hadley Joy." She smiled. "Who wants to be first?"

"I do," Mary Rose said, "I want to get it over with." She stood and followed Jessi down the hall.

"Way too much perky for me," Calamity said, looking after Jessi.

"Dick Cheney has way too much perky for you," Hadley joked, and she gave Calamity a friendly punch on the arm.

In just a few minutes Mary Rose returned, followed by Jessi with her clipboard. Hadley stood up, then followed the young nurse down the hall.

Robbie was next, then Calamity stood up slowly, glared at them and followed Jessi through the door.

"Not too bad," Hadley said.

"Same old, same old," Robbie said.

"I just hope they hurry and tell us the results," Mary Rose sighed. "I'm so darned anxious!"

A sharp yell shot through the room from behind the door they had all walked through. They looked at each other.

"She kicked the nurse again," Hadley said.

When Hard News Comes Calling

They waited. Mary Rose made three trips to the bathroom. "I have to pee a lot," she said.

"I like what the comedian Wanda Sykes said," Robbie smiled. "When I was young I used to carry clean panties in my purse in case I got lucky. Now I carry clean panties in my purse in case I sneeze."

"And we all have to remember our SHIT, especially at times like this," Mary Rose said. Even though they were all sitting down, they straightened their shoulders, held their heads high, looked straight ahead and pulled in their tummies. No slouching just because you're having some anxiety.

Jessi walked in through a different door, smiled at them, handed Calamity a note and looked at Robbie. "Robinson, please follow me. Your test results are back." Robbie hurried after her.

"What's the note say, Calamity?" Mary Rose asked.

"Ha!" Calamity said. "It says, 'Mammogram reading failed. Please make another appointment.' Like that's gonna happen!"

In just minutes, Robbie returned, gave them a thumbs up and Jessi called Hadley in. "Why aren't they calling me?" Mary Rose asked. "I went first."

Hadley came back smiling and they waited longer. "Oh boy," Mary Rose said. "Not good."

Several minutes later, Jessi came through the door, smiled at them and asked Mary Rose to follow her. They waited. After about twenty minutes, Jessi came out again. "Mary Rose asked me to let you know that she's having a biopsy. It will take about two hours. You can leave and call in to find out when she's finished if you want, or you can wait right here." Her smile was warm and genuine.

They walked slowly down the hall and took the elevator from the cancer center into the big hospital. Following signs, they finally arrived at the cafeteria. They didn't speak as they went through the beverage line and got soft drinks.

Hadley sighed. "There are so many questions. Chemotherapy? Mastectomy? Lumpectomy? Double mastectomy to be safe? Reconstruction? Prognosis? Support groups? Side effects of whatever? All those sound like dirty words to me right now. BUT", she added. "We don't even know if it's bad news yet." The others nodded.

Robbie turned her glass around on the table. "They're good here. They'll give her a lot of patient education."

Hadley sighed. "At least there is better anesthesia, better chemo, and more chances for survival."

They fell silent.

After nearly an hour, they walked out into the hospital garden, through the hallways and around the grounds; anything to make time pass. Finally, Hadley called the number Jessi had given them.

"Give us ten more minutes and she'll be done. Come back now if you want. We just made fresh coffee."

They went back.

When Mary Rose came through the door they all stood up. She was pale and looked as if she might faint. "It's cancer," she whispered. "They already have me scheduled for surgery."

"Crap!" Calamity said.

"Oh, Mary Rose," Robbie cried.

"I'm so sorry, Mary Rose," Hadley said and they hugged her

"Well, not much to do but hope for the best," Mary Rose said.

"Hey, Girl," Hadley said as they walked through the big doors leading from the cancer center. "We're here. You will never be alone in this, you hear?" Mary Rose nodded.

"We're Calamity's Angels," Robbie said, taking her little angel out of her slacks pocket. Calamity pulled her angel out of her jeans. "Got mine," she said. Hadley's silver angel was in her palm, shining in the bright sun. Mary Rose stopped walking and reached into her slacks pocket. Her face grew even paler. "Oh, no!" she said. "My angel's gone and I know I put it in there this morning. I wanted it for good luck and I always stick it in this pocket. Now I've lost my angel." Tears were welling up in her eyes. She reached into her pocket as deep as she could. She looked as if she might start to seriously cry, then she broke into a smile. "Whew!" she said, showing them the little angel in her palm. "Deep pockets. It turned into a crotch angel."

Mary Rose spoke as soon as they got in their big Hummer "They answered all my questions and gave me all this literature." Mary Rose held up a thick packet. "They're nice. I like my two doctors and the nurses. That means a lot." She looked dazed.

"Hey! Lunch in the Old Market is still on," Hadley said. "Mary Rose, you pick the restaurant."

That first night after the diagnosis was the worst. Mary Rose assured them she was fine and just wanted to rest. "Now that I know what has to be done, I can maybe get some sleep. I'm going to take a nap. See you at dinner." And she had headed to her apartment.

Hadley and Robbie put on their walking shoes and walked for an hour, their heads often moving close together as they talked. Calamity just disappeared.

Mary Rose didn't show up for dinner. Calamity ate faster than usual. Hadley moved food around on her plate. Robbie seemed to be chewing each bite twenty-two times. Finally Hadley laid her fork down. "I'm going to check on her." Robbie and Calamity stood up at the same time and hurried down the hall with Hadley.

"Mary Rose, it's us," Hadley said, ringing the doorbell at Mary Rose's apartment. There was a shuffling inside and the door opened. Mary Rose looked terrible. She was wearing a fluffy pink bathrobe, pink slippers and her face was close to matching both robe and slippers. Her cheeks were blotchy. Red spots appeared on her neck and forehead and her hair looked as if she'd tossed and turned. She had obviously been crying. A wad of tissue was clutched in her hand.

Mary Rose let them in, then sat down at her small kitchen table, her elbows on the table and her head in her hands. She began to cry. "I don't feel pretty anymore. And I worked so hard to be pretty." She collapsed her elbows onto the table, laid her head on her arms and sobbed. Tears welled up in Hadley's and Robbie's eyes and Calamity turned sideways.

They were quiet for a while. "Okay, that's it," Hadley said. "This calls for action. Mary Rose, get out your laptop." Mary Rose looked at her, blew her nose and walked over to a small desk to grab her computer. "Robbie," Hadley said, "Head for the coffee pot, we need coffee. Calamity," Hadley looked at Calamity and tried to think of something for the little spy to do. "Just stay where you are."

Mary Rose sat her laptop on the table and took a seat in front of it. Robbie was grinding fresh coffee beans and Calamity was staying where she was. Hadley stood behind Mary Rose. "We're going to write a letter to your email list. This is what I did when I had my cancer surgery. When we have a crisis in our lives we need as much help as we can get. It's always easier if you let people know what's going on instead of hiding it. Learning to ask for help and support is one of life's greatest lessons." She pulled a chair around so she could sit at one side and just behind Mary Rose. "I wrote a note to my email list and asked them to hold my hand. We're going to get you enough hands to paper a wall."

An hour later, the coffee pot was empty. From inside Mary Rose's refrigerator Calamity had dug out a package of Mrs. Goldberg's cinnamon rolls. Only crumbs were left on the napkins they had used as plates. "Okay, Mary Rose," Hadley said. "It looks good from here. Read it to us."

Mary Rose leaned toward the screen and read:

"I have some hard news to share. I have breast cancer. I know if you could be here you would hold my hand, but since you can't, I want to ask you to trace your hand on a piece of paper. Inside that hand, write me a note, and around the margins and on the back of the paper, send me your favorite jokes so those who wait the long wait while I'm in surgery will have something to smile about. And as I recover, I'll have something to smile about, too. Send them to me along with a truly tasteless get well card and I promise to smile at that as well. Send me good thoughts and if you pray, prayers are welcome. Thanks to all of you for caring about me."

And she listed the date of her surgery, her address and her phone number.

"That is brilliant," Robbie said.

"Got to hand it to both of you," Calamity said, nodding at Hadley and Mary Rose. She began cleaning up the napkins and crumbs.

Hadley looked at Mary Rose. "One or all of us should stay here tonight. Things really will look better in the morning. I know. Been there, done that, got the t-shirt to prove it."

Mary Rose nodded and smiled a soft smile. Her face had cleared up and her eyes looked brighter. "I know, Hadley, and I appreciate that. I think I would like someone with me tonight." Hadley and Robbie looked at each other and smiled, then they looked at Calamity. "But," Mary Rose continued, standing up and smiling a shy smile, "I'd like it to be Wiley."

They looked at her, their eyes wide and their eyebrows lifting. Mary Rose blushed in a rather attractive way. "We don't fool around, actually," she said. "Not that it's anybody's business, but we don't need a lot of sex anymore. I read where after your hormones stop moaning, you have what they call, 'decreased desire,'" She bent over a little and gave a little laugh. "But boy does that man know how to cuddle!"

Hadley began to laugh. "I hear you," she said. "Wes says anyone who thinks intimacy is all about sex doesn't know what real intimacy is."

"When you're young you think about sex all the time," Robbie added. "Now we have room for some creative thoughts to get into our heads." They looked at Calamity.

"Crap," Calamity said.

Robbie held up her hand. "Probably not the greatest time to ask this question, but what is Wiley's story, Mary Rose? He's a tremendously nice guy and he never ever talks about himself or his history."

Mary Rose sighed and shook her head. "I really don't know, Robbie. He hasn't talked to me, either. But one night I woke up because he was crying in his sleep. And I've heard him cry in the shower." She laughed a little laugh. "Either that, or he's a really bad singer!" Then Mary Rose reached for her cell phone and punched in a speed-dial number. Hadley and Robbie hugged her and turned toward the door. Calamity moved to the kitchen, rinsed out the coffee cups and put them in the cupboard. She turned, gave Mary Rose a quick, uncomfortable hug and headed toward the door after the other two.

"Sleep tight," Hadley said.

"We love you," Robbie said.

Calamity hesitated. "It's going to be all right," she said. Then, as she turned toward the door Robbie was pulling open for her, she added a soft, "Crap."

They hadn't gone far down the hall before they met Wiley walking fast toward them. He wasn't wearing his Stetson, but he moved his hand toward his forehead as if to tip his hat. "Ladies," he said, and he hurried on toward Mary Rose's open door.

Wiley Vondra went inside Mary Rose's apartment and walked into a warm hug. Hadley Joy Morris-Whitfield went inside her apartment, sat at her computer, went to her email and requested traced hands and jokes for a friend whom she loved; then she put on her jammies, poured a glass of good Chardonnay, crawled onto her bed, sat cross-legged and called Wes Longbow.

Robinson Leary went inside her apartment, turned on her computer and asked everyone on her email list to trace their hands and send jokes for a friend whom she loved; then she put on her jammies, grabbed the little black teddy bear that had recordings of the beloved voices of her mother and husband sewn into her paws, crawled under her covers, buried her head in the little bear and cried.

Calamity Doodles just went inside.

A One-Breasted Amazon

In both Greek and Roman mythology there appeared a band of Warrior Women, the Amazons. They were associated with the very highest gods. They went into battle with fierce courage and determination. Their loyalty was to the gods, their battle and especially to each other. Some of these Amazon warriors, legends say, cut off one breast so they could better hold and shoot their deadly arrows from massive bows. They were one tough breed of home girl. Such a woman was Mary Rose McGill who was once shy, plain, dowdy and hopeless. Mary Rose McGill was turning into an Amazon.

"I read this really great book before I had my cancer surgery," Hadley was saying. They were seated around a table in the surgery waiting room, coffee cups in hand, cinnamon rolls at the ready, beginning the long wait while Mary Rose's breast was removed and her lymph nodes examined. "It's called *Close to the Bone* by a Jungian psychologist named Jean Shinoba Bolen. She compares the operating room to a temple that has been cleansed and prepared in a sacred rite just for you, where the docs and nurses represent special servants who wear temple garb and await you, where you are put into a deep trance and these servants minister to you. When you come out of that sacred room, something has been removed from you, a scar marks your sacrifice and you are changed forever." She looked at the ceiling and shook her head. "I wish I could remember it better, but when I looked for the book to give to Mary Rose I couldn't find it."

"Read a joke," Calamity said impatiently. Calamity had disappeared after that night in Mary Rose's apartment, but she had mysteriously reappeared in time for the surgery. This time she had looked tired and had seemed frustrated on the drive bringing Mary Rose to the hospital.

"Okay," Robbie said. They brought the traced hands and jokes in two briefcases. After all their email requests and letting other residents at Meadow Lakes know what they were doing, Mary Rose had received over three hundred pieces of paper with hands traced on them. A good friend of Hadley's, who had only one arm, had asked a friend to trace her hand. There were sheets of colored paper, paper with designs and pages and pages of encouraging notes. Nick, a young man, whom Hadley loved like a son, had glued a yellow rubber kitchen glove to a sheet of green paper to represent his hand. He had attached a pink 'Panic Button' and written, "Don't panic, Mary Rose, it will be okay."

People hadn't just written jokes in the margins by their hands or on the back of the paper. They'd gone on the internet and collected joke after joke. Now the girls sat with stacks of paper in front of them taking turns reading. They were smiling and every now and then laughed. Other people in the waiting room were listening and laughing as well.

Robbie adjusted her glasses and began to read. "I was getting out of shape so I joined an exercise class. I twisted, gyrated, jumped up and down and sweat like crazy. But by the time I got my leotards on, the class was over." She shrugged.

Calamity almost smiled. "I've got a future BOOB Girl," she said, and she lifted the paper up where she could see it better. "A kindergarten teacher told her class they could draw anything they wanted. One little girl was really intense and drawing as fast as she could. The teacher went over to her desk. 'What are you drawing?' she asked the little girl.

'A picture of God,' the little girl replied.

'You know, Honey, no one really knows what God looks like,' the teacher said.

'Well, they will in a minute!' the little girl said."

"Ha!" Hadley said, "I got a medical one. 'An older doc brings in a young doc to help in his practice. One day Mrs. Wilson comes in and goes to see the young doc. A few minutes later she comes running out of his examination room screaming hysterically. She dashes down the hall into the arms of the old doctor who takes her into another room, calms her down and after a few minutes he storms into the young doc's office. The young doctor is sitting at his desk, clipboard in his lap, writing something. 'Mrs. Wilson is sixty-two years old,' the old doc says, 'why in the world did you tell her she was pregnant?' The young doc doesn't even look up. 'Tell me,' he says, 'does she still have those hiccups she came in to have cured?'"

They read on. Other people who were waiting, watching their watches and drinking coffee didn't just listen to the jokes being read. Several came to the table where the three friends sat, heard a joke or two, smiled, talked about their person who was experiencing their own crisis or life-threatening illness. "It never stops, does it?" Robbie had asked, looking around at the anxious faces. Even with the jokes, it was a rather dismal day. The weather was threatening rain. "Sometimes the sky just needs a good cry," Robbie sighed, looking out the window and quoting the old children's song. "Rain, rain, rain," Hadley said softly. Robbie finished with, "Then the sun comes out and shines again."

"Whoopee," Calamity growled.

Robert, Rueben, Leonard and Clyde came by to keep them company for an hour. Robert immediately pulled out his Bible and said he wanted to offer a prayer. They bowed their heads, "Grant me the senility to forget the people I never liked anyway, to run into the ones I do like and the eyesight to know the difference." They looked up, grins on their faces. Calamity uttered a soft, "Crap," and Robert bowed. "The Senility Prayer,"

Rueben gave each of the girls, including Calamity a hug. It felt good to stand up and stretch and get a good hug. Clyde delivered a huge basket of cinnamon rolls which he placed on a table in the center of the waiting room and invited everyone there to have one. After they had all looked at Clyde, then Leonard in his white outfit and aluminum hat, then back to Clyde's green and yellow wedgies, no one moved, even though the scent of the rolls was tempting. Finally Calamity moved toward the basket and took a roll.

"The most delicious thing you've ever tasted," she said, taking a bite, "and a special flavoring in them reduces anxiety." The people in the waiting room seemed to rise from their chairs all at the same time. In less than forty seconds the basket was empty and the receptionist was making fresh pots of coffee.

Nothing Feels Good Like Feeling Good

Mary Rose had good news from her surgery. Everything looked good and she would probably only need a short round of chemotherapy. She awoke from surgery fairly alert and everyone was relieved it was over. Her four daughters, Mary

Claire, Mary Ruth, Mary Elizabeth and Mary
Louise all came and then all went.

As for the other three BOOB Girls, they were on a
mission. Three pairs of legs marched out the doors
of Meadow Lakes Retirement Community toward
the big Hummer waiting in the parking lot. Three
doors opened at the same time and Robbie burned
rubber going out of the driveway.

They shot down the street to fifty-first and Center
Street and into the parking lot of Kubat's Pharmcy,
one of the few family-owned drugstores left in the
city. Hadley, a large, colorful shopping bag under
her arm, rushed inside. In just minutes, she rushed
out again and climbed into the Hummer. They
drove down Center Street to eighty-fourth, turned
left and in minutes were parked at David M.
Mangelsen's well-equipped variety and hobby store.

Three Hummer doors opened at the same time.
Three pairs of legs climbed out and marched into
the store. Hadley's shopping back was bulging as it
swung back and forth.

Inside, Robbie headed past an attractive display of scented candles while Calamity and Hadley hurried to the fabric section where Marla Mangelsen and two craft instructors were waiting with a glue gun.

Twenty minutes later, three pairs of legs climbed back into the Hummer and three car doors closed at the same time. The big machine rolled out of the parking lot and headed toward the hospital.

If the Hat Fits, Wear it

Mary Rose was sitting up in bed wearing a lavender bed jacket and a big smile when her friends walked through the door. They were puffing just a little as they gathered around her bed. "Here ya go, girl," Hadley said, handing her the shopping bag. Mary Rose opened it, pulled out her gift and began to laugh.

"It's a hat made out of a bedpan!" she squealed. "The nurses have to see this." She pushed her call button and put the hat on her head. The bedpan had been transformed, covered with fuzzy pink fabric and decorated with daisies and ribbons. Mary Rose put it gently on top of her blonde hair. A nurse hurried through the door, stopped short, began to laugh then rushed outside to call her colleagues. Mary Rose eased out of bed and into the bathroom to look in the mirror. She laughed again.

Mary Rose was wearing the bedpan hat when her three friends walked with her out the front doors of the hospital toward the black Hummer waiting in the patient pick-up area. A nurse was pushing the wheelchair required of everyone being discharged. Mary Rose was thanking her for being a great nurse and for taking pictures of her in the hat. "This is one powerhouse lady," the nurse said, turning toward Hadley. Hadley nodded and smiled. Mary Rose stood, hugged the nurse and turned toward the passenger door Hadley was holding open for her. Mary Rose looked at her three friends. "Just look at us," she said. "We're slumped over like old biddies. SHIT!" And they looked at Mary Rose, straightened their shoulders, lifted their heads and tucked in their tummies. Then they got in the Hummer and headed home.

Bald is Beautiful

Mary Rose's toughness only lasted a day or two, then she was back to normal. She was taking it easy and the other three helped by holding movie marathons featuring westerns one day, romantic comedies the next, action adventures, and a full *Batman* series where they compared the actors, sets and directors.

"I never did get this Robin-as-kid-sidekick thing," Robbie said after the last movie was shown and they were walking down the hall toward the dining room for dinner. Suddenly Calamity stopped. "Wait a minute!" They stopped. She was thinking and mumbling to herself.

"I remembered it, listen up. Batman and Robin go camping. They find a nice spot and set up their tent, crawl in and go to sleep. All at once Batman wakes Robin up, 'Robin! Look up! What do you see?' Robin looks up and says, 'I see millions of stars, Batman.' Batman says, 'But what does that tell you?' Robin says, 'Astronomically it tells me there are millions of galaxies and perhaps millions of planets, astrologically it tells me Saturn is in Pluto, chronologically it appears to be about a quarter past three and theologically it tells me God is all mighty and all powerful and it looks like it's going to be a nice day tomorrow. What does it tell you, Batman?" Batman looks at him and says, 'Robin, you idiot, somebody stole our tent.'"

"Oh geez what a groaner. At least a cow didn't come by and poop on the Robin," Robbie said.

"Mary Rose shook her head. "It's a knick-knack Patty Whack, give the frog a loan."

They laughed their way down the long hallway to the dining room. Dinner that night was vegetable lasagna with a delicious tossed salad. They thoroughly enjoyed it.

If the Wig Fits, Wear It, too

Peyton Claireborne himself was pouring the champagne, and he was wearing a tuxedo. The tall, black, hair stylist had brought in a massive bouquet of mixed flowers and set out two trays of exotic cheeses and crackers. Mary Rose McGill was getting her head shaved before she started chemotherapy. She was in Peyton's styling chair, looking into his large mirror, pink stylist's apron tied snuggly behind her neck. Robbie, Hadley and Calamity were on other stylist's chairs watching and sipping their champagne from outrageously expensive flute glasses.

"I said goodbye to my breast before the surgery," Mary Rose was explaining to Peyton. "I thanked it for helping make me a woman, for nursing my babies, for a lot of enjoyment in my life. Then I told it something was terribly wrong inside it and it had to be removed. Cried like a baby when I did it. I was looking at it in the mirror, talking and crying."

"I said goodbye to my uterus," Hadley added. "Those are rituals…like this is…and they're important. They complete our lives and honor what's precious to us."

Robbie smiled and nodded. "I tell my heart it will be okay when it acts up and I ritualize things by writing poetry about what's happening to me."

"Crap," Calamity said.

Peyton pulled out his razor and turned it on. He handed Robbie four pink silk ribbons and spoke to her in a very authoritative voice. "When Peyton hands you a strand of Mary Rose's hair, darling," he said, "you must carefully tie a ribbon around it. Make sure the bows are exactly the same size. Each of you will have a strand of this delicious hair styled and designed by Peyton himself." Peyton was one of Omaha's most beautiful drag queens, openly gay and proud and with one of the most successful businesses in the Old Market. In addition to looking outstanding in a tux, Peyton had another thing going for him. He, along with his friend Troy, owner of the One Drake Place Salon and Spa, provided free wigs and makeovers for clients undergoing cancer treatment. Mary Rose had picked out her wig, a near-match to her own hair.

But before Mary Rose sat down in front of the big mirror, her three friends had slipped into Peyton's wig salon and now they sat behind her on the styling chairs that he had pulled over for them. They were looking very different.

Hadley was wearing a long red-haired wig that curled around her shoulders. Robbie wore blonde braids and Calamity's head was covered with bright pink spikes. "It so fits you, darling," Peyton had said. The razor hummed, Robbie bound strands of hair in the ribbons while Mozart played softly in the background. Soon Mary Rose McGill looked in the mirror at a reflection showing perfect makeup and beautiful hair.

"Peyton it's beautiful!" she exclaimed, tears forming in her eyes.

"We have a present," Robbie sang and she pulled a bright package out from behind her chair. Mary Rose opened it and pulled out six brightly colored and patterned scarves. "For when you don't want to wear the wig," Hadley explained.

"You know," Mary Rose said during their lunch at Mark's Bistro, a trendy little café on their way back to Meadow Lakes. They were sitting outside under a huge tree that canopied one level of Mark's terraced patio. Around them other diners laughed and visited. One well-dressed lady had complimented Mary Rose on her "lovely hair style" as she passed them on her way to another table. "I thought this would be a terrible thing," Mary Rose continued, "but I've got to say I've learned a heck of a lot. I've learned about courage and composure and trust. I've learned how to advocate for myself. I've learned that I am loved. I knew that, but it really came home to me through all this."

"It can be a really good spiritual experience," Hadley said. "It took me a long time to say my cancer experience was a 'good' experience, but it was. And I found four words for who I wanted to be: Grace. Humor. Courage and Confidence."

"I learned never to be arrogant about my health," Robbie said. "My heart t taught me to be a lot more understanding of people with physical problems."

"We're not here for a long time," Calamity said. "We're here for a good time. Live life, ladies!" They agreed and raised their glasses of iced tea in salute. It felt, for the first and perhaps only time, that Calamity Doodles was a BOOB Girl.

Clown Down, Girls and Boys

Chemotherapy was administered in one large room at the cancer center. Seven oversized, comfortable reclining chairs were in a line facing ceiling-to-floor windows overlooking a small lake with five fountains in the center. There were small televisions attached to each chair so people could put on headphones, turn on the set and watch whatever they wanted without bothering other patients. A customized tray attached to each chair welcomed the use of IPads and laptop computers. Soft music played over a speaker system and if you wanted privacy, there were beds and chairs with curtains to block out the world. Nurses in colorful uniforms were checking on the people in the chairs, some of whom were reading, some of whom were watching their TVs and some of whom were just napping or staring out the windows.

"You could have a pedicure in these things," Hadley remarked when they first saw the chairs.

"You could become addicted to soaps," Robbie said, looking at the attached TVs.

"Crap," Calamity said.

Mary Rose waved them off. "Go forth and enjoy yourselves," she told them. "I'm catching up on my reading and relaxing." She waved her latest romance novel at them. "I'll call you when I'm done." They left.

"Wait a minute," Calamity said when they reached the big atrium lobby. She looked surprisingly shy. "I don't do this, at least I don't do it very damn much or very damn well, but I'll tell you, girls, that place needs help."

"You mean the chemo lounge?" Hadley asked.

"I thought it was very nice," Robbie said, a note of surprise in her voice.

"Oh, it was nice…and efficient…and sterile…and way too peaceful." She moved closer to them. "Here's what we're going to do," she said.

The next time they brought Mary Rose to the cancer center they dropped her off, saying they had some errands to run. She had still been in the shower when Hadley and Robbie helped Calamity load two large suitcases into the back of the Hummer and she hadn't seen the four BOOB Boys and Wiley drive out of the Meadow Lakes parking lot, Rueben's Jesus Van spitting smoke from the tailpipe. She didn't even notice that same van parked in the cancer center parking lot with the head of a friendly troll sticking out the window watching her. Mary Rose didn't even think the chemotherapy staff seemed unusually cheery and watchful that day.

Mary Rose was settled into her big recliner, hooked up to the IV running the drugs into her system. She had gotten through two more chapters of her book when the door to the chemo room crashed open. Eight colorful, bright, crazy-looking clowns burst in. Circus music was blaring from a boom box balanced on the shoulders of a midget and the tallest and strangest was carrying a gigantic basket of cinnamon rolls.

Mary Rose put her hand to her mouth and began to laugh so hard she started to cry. All the other patient's eyes grew wide and they pulled off their headphones and leaned forward to see what was going on. One of the clowns was passing out red clown noses to each patient and staff member and they were all putting them on. Mary Rose laughed harder. "I have to pee!" she yelled between giggles.

"Remember," Calamity had told them earlier, "you're not clowns. I'm the only one who can officially have a name and clown down. For all of you, this is like Halloween. You're just dressed up." It had taken just one phone call from Calamity and the suitcases and clown paraphernalia had appeared at her door.

They had gathered in the chaplain's office as soon as Mary Rose disappeared behind the big automatic doors. The chaplain, a friend of Hadley's, had made the arrangements and now her staff watched as clowns appeared before them. When they left the office, big clown feet flopping, and headed for the chemotherapy lounge, the chaplain's entire staff followed, leaving the answering machine in charge of the pastoral care department.

"There are few things more terrifying than a clown," Robert quoted.

"Stephen King from *It*?" Robbie said.

"No, it's from me. I was always afraid of clowns. Stephen King said, 'Hey-ho, let's go!'" And they went, bursting into a room full of people attached to machines and smiling surprised smiles.

Clyde was cute as a bug, mainly because he was dressed as a bug; a big, frightening lady bug complete with antennae, huge red shoes, painted red face and red clown nose. Robert looked like a deranged undertaker with an oversized black suit, oversized red polka dot bowtie, crooked top hat with red hair sticking out from under it and a white face with bright red cheeks. Rueben was dressed as a scarecrow with fake straw sticking out his sleeves and pant legs. Leonard was dressed as he usually dressed, all in white with his aluminum hat. He fit right in ... with both clowns and the medical staff.

Hadley and Robbie were twin ballerinas in ugly tutus, pink tights and body suits that had so many outlandish sequins they hid their love handles. Huge pink ribbons adorned their rainbow-colored fright wigs and there were bright red circles on their cheeks; circles the same color as their clown noses. Wiley was in full cowboy regalia complete with massive fake cardboard Hopalong Cassidy guns and holsters that came down to his knees.

But Calamity was something else. It was obvious her costume was authentic. It was made up of all the colors of the rainbow. Her red tights actually complimented the red, white and blue high top sneakers. Her frilly skirt twirled and moved and her long-sleeved shirt boasted a really elaborate neck scarf. Her wig was made up of blonde Shirley Temple curls with a tasteful bow on top. Her makeup made her look like a teenager escaped from a 1950's prom disaster. Everyone in the chairs, along with the staff began to applaud.

Robert pulled out a sponge mallet on a stick, threw another to Rueben and they began a mallet fight. The other clowns began a macabre dance with Clyde spinning in between and around them and falling down. The five men clowns sang "Sweet Adeline" in horrendous four and occasionally five part harmony. Clyde followed a doctor step for step all around the room and to each chair, both of them shaking each patient's hand while Clyde made goo-goo eyes at all the women and actually pinched the behind of one pretty nurse. The nurse bent over, spread his antennae and kissed his head, causing him to drop to the floor in a pretend faint.

For nearly half an hour no one moved and everyone laughed. The act ended with an acrobatic display by Calamity. She did back flips, somersaults, cartwheels and added dance moves. The audience ooohed and ahhhhhed and clapped. She was good. Right up until the finale when she did the splits.

She spread her legs, raised her arms and landed on the floor with a splat, legs extended straight out in front and in back. She smiled. She nodded. She looked around, her eyes growing large. She didn't move. Everyone applauded and still she didn't move. She just sat there on the floor, her legs straight out in the splits, her hands high in the air, making strange motions with her head and hands.

"I think she wants us to come over there," Robbie whispered. Hadley nodded and motioned with her head toward Rueben. The three of them improvised a funny little dance and began to prance around Calamity, bending over so they could hear her.

"I'm stuck, dammit! Do something," she growled. They looked at each other and shrugged a panicked little shrug.

Rueben danced around behind her, grabbed her under her arms, whispered, "Keep your arms straight out," and lifted her into the air. Hadley and Robbie danced over and opened the door. Doing a weird two-step shuffle, Rueben carried Calamity, legs still in split position, out through the open door. Applause and laughter followed them.

In the hallway, Rueben held Calamity up as high as he could. Hadley, Robbie and two chaplains gently pulled her legs down and she stood up, a little unsteady and with a firm grip on Rueben.

"That was fun. And crap!" she said, rubbing her hips.

In the chaplain's office they laughed, removed their makeup and congratulated themselves on a good performance. Calamity was stretching and rubbing her legs. "I'm getting too old for this shit," she said, and both Hadley and Robbie straightened their shoulders, held their heads high and tucked in their tummies, without even thinking about it.

"That, I believe," Robert said, "is a quote by Jack Nicholas in *The Bucket List* but I'm sure he's not the first."

Robbie knew the source. "It's from the good old movie *Lethal Weapon*. Danny Glover says it."

At dinner that night Mary Rose laughed till she cried again. "I was so glad I didn't pee right there in the chair," she giggled. "And I went just before I sat down, but you were so funny."

"It was all Calamity's idea and choreography," Rueben told her. They had pulled two tables together so all the clowns could celebrate together.

"I was the cutest," Clyde said.

"For a troll," Mary Rose added and patted his knee.

"Calamity?" Robert asked. "You were a real clown. What was your clown's name?"

Calamity was quiet for a few seconds, then she looked around at all of them and in a small voice said, "I was Sweet Sweet Pea."

After dinner Calamity disappeared again and was gone for more than a week.

Part Four

Gated Communities

*If we have to die, I want to die with my eyes closed
and my heart open*
Robert, quoting from *The Bucket List*

And with my knees together.
Hadley Joy Morris-Whitfield

And in clean underwear
Mary Rose McGill

Crap!
Calamity Doodles

*For all those men who say, "Why buy the cow when
you can get the milk for free?" Here's an update for
you. Nowadays 80% of women are against
marriage. Why? Because women realize it's not
worth buying an entire pig just to get a little
sausage!* Andy Rooney

Calamity rushed into the dining room just as the others sat down with full plates from the luncheon buffet. She plopped into her chair and leaned in on her elbows toward the middle of the table.

"The action when we robbed the grave with the BOOB Boys finally paid off. We found the necklace hidden in the casket and we caught my ex." She was out of breath and excited. "Henry, my sixth, cooperated. We don't know who has the microchip, but we know who knows and he doesn't know we know."

"Say what?" Robbie and Hadley said together.

Mary Rose leaned forward. "He squealed. He gave it up. He came clean. He spilled the beans. He lightened his load. I love cop talk." She smiled at Calamity. "And spy talk, too, of course." She thought for a second. "And Bruce Willis," she mumbled.

Hadley pushed her plate toward Calamity, handed her a fork and the little spy speared a piece of meat and began to chew. "The guy who knows who has it? His name is Boogie 'Bad Boy' Boyer. He's been a runner for the mob. Henry says he delivered the chip and now all we need to do is to get sweet old Boogie to tell us who has it and where it is."

"Where is this Boogie man?" Robbie asked.

"Lives in a gated community," Calamity said, sticking her fork into one of Hadley's string beans.

Hadley nodded. "I know those communities. Most are the McMansions in West Omaha. Which subdivision does this Mr. Boyer call home?"

"The Omaha Regional Correctional Center. His gated community is the prison."

Never Cross A Prison Warden

Calamity was a genius when it came to intrigue and planning. They were at a table on the Meadow Lakes patio discussing how they could get Boogie Boyer to "spill the beans" and tell them where the chip was stashed. Mary Rose was in seventh heaven with spy, cop and intrigue talk.

"One of us will visit him in jail," Calamity was saying. "Pretend to be a church lady, Boogie is very religious. We'll do the missionary thing."

"Let me go! Let me go! I've always wanted to do something like this! I'll take cinnamon rolls!" Mary Rose said. "I've had cancer. I deserve to play detective!"

Hadley looked at her with shocked amusement. "Mary Rose! Get a life. You want a pity favor?"

Mary Rose looked back at her and didn't blink.

"Crap!" Calamity said. "Mary Rose, you get to go because you look like the most innocent and you know church talk. The agency will clear it with the prison warden, but you have to really be with the program. The warden is tough. One screw-up and we're outta there, understand?" Mary Rose nodded. She was still in chemotherapy, but the only side-effect was some expected fatigue. She felt good and she looked good. They began to make plans to meet Mr. Boogie Bad Boy Boyer in his gated community and literally loosen his tongue with Mrs. Goldberg's cinnamon rolls.

Now the time had come. They sat in the Hummer outside the prison. A huge campus, the complex was surrounded by an eight-foot high fence topped with rolls of barbed wire. A strong wind blew dust across the yard and into the parking lot. They could see several well-built inmates lifting weights in a fenced-in area off to one side. Others were in a small smoking area and still more were walking from one building to another. They all wore dark brown slacks, brown shirts and brown shoes.

"I thought they all wore orange," Hadley said.

"They're actually mostly good looking, too," Robbie noticed.

Mary Rose sat in the passenger seat, dressed in a pale green suit, light tan two-inch heels and expensive panty hose. A delicate cross hung on a chain around her neck and a small angel adorned her label. She was clutching six cinnamon rolls wrapped in plastic. Robert's Bible was tucked into her purse for good luck, credibility and inspiration.

The girls consulted Mrs. Goldberg about getting cinnamon rolls into the prison and Mrs. Goldberg told her nephews. Clyde had stood before them that morning with a big grin and the holey Holy Bible.

"Robert is tied up in the library looking for more quotes," Clyde had told them as he presented the Bible. "He wanted you to have this for today." The book proudly displayed the hole Clyde had shot into it at Peyton's grave. "Robert also said to tell you, 'Mix a little silliness into your serious plans. It is good to be silly at the right moment.'" Then he had turned to Robbie. "Robert also said you wouldn't believe it, but that's a quote direct from the philosopher, Horace."

"I wouldn't believe it," Robbie had said.

"Here's the deal," Calamity explained, "even in the visiting rooms, only food that comes *from* prison and is wrapped in plastic is allowed. Nothing weird is getting to a prisoner on this warden's watch."

Mrs. Goldberg had just laughed.

"Remember girls," Evangeline Goldberg told them, "my family knows the mob and I know the cook at the prison. He killed another man with a large carving knife." She looked off into the distance. "Now he's a cook. I guess he always liked kitchen work." She nodded. "He'll tell me how to fix those rolls." She struggled up from her oversized easy chair and pounded her way out to the kitchen.

She returned immediately with a plate of cinnamon rolls in one hand and the coffee pot in the other. "Here you go," she said. "Help yourselves."

They had helped themselves. Now they were sitting in the Hummer, staring at the prison, located close to the Omaha airport and next door to a homeless shelter. Since the day was cloudy and windy, Mary Rose had added extra hairspray to her wig.

There was no silliness now as Calamity pointed toward the guest entrance to the prison. "Go girl. Just do everything the warden says. Remember, nobody crosses the warden." Mary Rose nodded, held the cinnamon rolls in front of her and slid off the seat and out of the Hummer. Robbie and Hadley gave her a little finger wave when she looked back. Calamity gave her a thumbs-up. "Probably the dumbest thing I've ever done, sending her in there. Goodbye Little Red Riding Hood. Hello Big Bad Wolf."

Mary Rose had role-played, rehearsed, memorized and studied. As she walked through the heavy doors into the prison reception area and looked around, she promptly forgot everything.

The receptionist was an attractive black woman who put down one of Dan Brown's books as Mary Rose came toward her desk. "May I help you?"

"I have an appointment with Warden Shurridge," Mary Rose squeaked, then she reminded herself sternly, *SHIT!* She straightened up, tucked it in and looked confident. The receptionist unlocked a large glass door behind her desk. The walls were glass as well and Mary Rose could see a muscular man in a dark suit sitting at a desk. *He looks tough all right.*

She followed the receptionist, paused at Dark Suit's desk and smiled at him. But the receptionist walked on, past two more big men at two more big desks toward an ornately carved wooden door that must have come from a prison built over one hundred years ago. The receptionist knocked softly on the door, then opened it. *Oh boy,* Mary Rose thought. *Here we go.* She stepped through the door.

Warden Shurridge

The office was beautiful. Live plants sat on a shelf under a large window overlooking the prison yard. Tom Mangelsen wildlife photographs, all of various owls, decorated the walls. Five comfortable chairs

160

sat in a semi-circle in front of an attractive wooden desk. Two young women stood as Mary Rose entered. A third woman, seated behind the desk, rose at the same time, walked around the desk and held out her hand.

"Hello, dear," she said. "I'm Warden Shurridge. Please call me Karen." Mary Rose was looking into the soft blue eyes of what appeared to be a sweet, gentle, gray-haired grandmother. The warden was attractive, short, comfortably round and from all appearances should have been wearing an apron and holding out a plate of cookies. Cookies, however, were on a delicate china plate on a console along with a silver coffeepot. Family photos took up the rest of the console and a colorful rug that covered nearly the entire floor made this one of the friendliest offices Mary Rose had seen.

"Thank you for helping us," Mary Rose said, and she smiled, first at the warden then at the two young women, one of whom was in full law-enforcement uniform complete with automatic pistol. The other, an attractive African American, was wearing a navy blue Coldwater Creek skirt and jacket. Beautiful braided cornrows covered her hair.

"This is Teresa," Warden Shurridge said, pointing to the blonde officer, "and this is Loretta. They'll show you where to go, bring Mr. Boyer to you and answer any questions you have. But it's nearly lunch time. We want you to have lunch with us and get acquainted. We always eat with the inmates."

Mary Rose nearly panicked. "Oh, I couldn't. It's really not necessary." She looked at their smiling faces. "I'm not hungry?" She squeaked.

"It's not a question, dear," the warden said, taking her arm with one hand and the cinnamon rolls with the other. She laid the plastic-wrapped rolls on her desk, turned Mary Rose toward the door and said, "Mr. Boyer will be at lunch and if he sees you with us, he'll be attentive. I'll also be able to let you talk to some of our other inmates so he won't be suspicious when you suddenly show up." She patted Mary Rose's arm. "We have a lot of church folk coming in here. We're making you part of the routine." Mary Rose nodded. The warden led the way out the door, pushing her glasses up on her nose as she began to walk. She spoke to everyone in the outer room and they all smiled and said something back to her. Mary Rose fell in beside Officer Teresa's revolver.

"Not what you expected was it?" Teresa said. Her gray shirt was ironed so sharply that creases stood out on the back. Her black shoes were shined to perfection and her badge reflected the lights as they moved down a long corridor.

"Not at all," Mary Rose said. "Who is Loretta?" The trim, attractive black woman was walking beside the warden, laughing and talking.

"She's the lieutenant in charge," Teresa answered. "If we have to have a lockdown, she pushes the button. If we have trouble, she ends it." Mary Rose nodded. This was not a Loretta who was one square short of a crazy quilt like the Meadow Lake librarian, Loretta Ripp. Thin and fit, this Loretta looked as if she could take down any prisoner who made trouble and never twist her pantyhose.

"What's the warden like?" Mary Rose asked.

"Everyone loves her," Teresa said. "She takes good care of her employees. She takes good care of our inmates. She's great. Nobody crosses her."

"That's what I've heard," Mary Rose muttered.

Boogie Bad Boy Boyer

Lunch wasn't bad. The buffet featured healthy food and Mary Rose only saw one cook wielding a kitchen knife over a turkey breast. Inmates passed their table, spoke almost reverently to the Warden, the officer and the lieutenant. The men were polite, mostly young, and an almost even mix of whites, blacks and browns.

After lunch, Teresa stood up and looked at Mary Rose. "Show time," she said. "I have to pat you down. I hope you didn't wear an underwire bra."

Mary Rose's eyes grew wide and she shook her head. "Oh, I'm not wired." She stammered. "I mean I'm not wearing a wire." She was becoming frustrated. "Dammit!" What I mean is, I don't think people should wear wires in their underwear!"

Teresa nodded. "I take that as a 'no.'"

The young officer led Mary Rose to a small room, ran her hands over her sides, arms and legs and asked Mary Rose to open her mouth. "Girls try to smuggle in rings and other things in their mouths," she said. Mary Rose nodded and opened wide.

I've always wanted to do something like this. I've always wanted to do something like this. Mary Rose kept saying inside her head. *I've always wanted to do something like this.*

"I won't make you take your wig off." Teresa smiled. "It's very nice by the way." She motioned with one hand. "Let's go, Mary Rose."

The door didn't slam shut and lock after Mary Rose when she went into the visiting room. She looked at

Teresa. "I thought I'd talk on a phone through a glass or something,"

Teresa grinned. "Not here."

She motioned to an orange plastic table with four matching chairs. There were five other such tables and chairs in the room. The whole place was surprisingly attractive, with large windows, a walkway over the top and windows in the ceilings. A guard watched from a glassed-in area filled with computers and communication equipment. Mary Rose sat in one of the chairs. Another officer appeared and handed Teresa the package of cinnamon rolls from the warden's office.

Mary Rose looked around. "What now?"

"Good luck."

Teresa and her gun and her pressed uniform turned and walked out, the door sliding open as she approached it. She nodded to the guard on duty and left Mary Rose totally and absolutely alone.

I've always wanted to do something like this.

In just a few minutes, another door slid open and a man walked in, saw Mary Rose, swaggered over to her table and sat down.

Mary Rose straightened up and cleared her throat. "I drew your name from my church group's Visit-A-Prisoner list, Mr. Boyer, and I brought you the best cinnamon rolls you've ever tasted."

Boogie looked at her and grunted. He wasn't an ugly man. He was around sixty years old with brown hair in a neat ponytail. His face was blank and wrinkled and he looked as if he spent a lot of time working out. Mary Rose tore open the plastic and handed him a cinnamon roll, realizing she'd forgotten to put napkins in her purse. He looked at the roll, grunted and took a big bite.

"I baked them just for you," Mary Rose lied. Boogie nodded approval. "I've never met a genuine, hardened criminal before," Mary Rose sighed and looked deep into Boogie's squinty gray eyes. There was a pause while Boogie finished the roll and

167

licked his fingers. Mary Rose handed him another.
"I don't suppose you'd let me hear you do some real
mob talk, would you?" Mary Rose looked innocent.
"Like what?" Boogie's voice was surprisingly high
and squeaky and sounded like a pre-pubescent
teenager was trapped somewhere inside him.

"Like what you'd say just before you shot
someone," Mary Rose said, still smiling.
Boogie smiled back, "I'd say, 'Ya had it comin.
Now eat my gun.'"

Mary Rose smiled her most charming smile and put
her right hand over her heart. "That was just
wonderful! Do say some more." She handed him
another roll. Boogie took a big bite. "OK, Coppers.
Bite the dust." He made a gun out of his thumb and
forefinger and pointed it at Mary Rose.

"I just love criminal talk." She handed him another
cinnamon roll, knowing he was headed for a good
sugar high. Boogie was taking bigger and bigger

bites, licking his fingers after each mouthful. "Get your dumb asses into the car and don't say nothin'!"

Bad Boy was on a roll -- literally. Mary Rose leaned forward, looked around and whispered. "If you really needed to hide something you'd stolen, where would a genius criminal like you hide it?" Boogie looked a little puzzled. "I might need to hide something someday," she whispered louder.

"I'd just get one of them safety deposit boxes."

'No, I need to keep an eye on it all the time. And it's very small, like one of those port things you put in a computer only even smaller." She actually batted her eyelashes and handed him another roll.

"Oh, like a microchip?"

"Shhhh! I've never told anyone but you." Mary Rose had never seen a microchip in her life. Boogie leaned as close to her as he could and stuffed half the cinnamon roll in his mouth. "Immf pudst it om schmorthing swmall." He swallowed.

"Excuse me?""

Boogie swallowed again and did another finger lick. "I'd put it on something small." He pointed to her fingernails. She had just had an acrylic fill from her nail tech, Wigs, at Peyton Claireborne's salon. Boogie smelled like sugar.

"This is called, *Blushingham Palace.*" She smiled.

"I really like that red one," he said shyly. "*I Am Not A Waitress.* It's from that company, OPI."

Mary Rose kept focused. "You'd put the chip in a bottle of nail polish?"

"Nope. I'd put it on the *bottom* of the bottle. Like a silver color where it would blend in, you know? Maybe that one called *Birthday Babe.* It's silver like the chip. You'd never notice, even if you turned it over to look at the label on the bottom. It would just look like a thick, blank nail polish label."

"You are so clever! I bet you even did that once." Boogie squared his shoulders. "Not me, but I know a dude who did."

Mary Rose gave him an enraptured gaze and handed him the last roll. Boogie held it for a minute so he could speak more clearly. Then he leaned toward Mary Rose. "He's like us. Very religious. Goes to some big church out around 204th Street. That's where I met him when I made a special delivery. This guy has a mansion out in West Omaha. I don't know where." He looked at her and smiled. There was a sprinkling of cinnamon roll crumbs on his lips and on the table. He licked his lips.

"He must have massive security," Mary Rose said, still hanging onto the sweet smile.

"Yeah. A system, walls all around and six mean guard dogs." Boogie grinned. Mary Rose could see two gold teeth. "Bad Boy, you've been so helpful."

Boogie looked suspicious again. "How you mean, 'helpful'?"

Mary Rose realized she'd slipped up. She leaned forward again and whispered. "I was so depressed, I didn't know what to do, and I really didn't want to come here. But you have given me one of the most exciting and interesting conversations I've ever had. I can't thank you enough." Mary Rose stood up. She smiled. Boogie stood up as well.

"Thanks, Lady. I don't even know your name."

"Nancy Hammerseth." Mary Rose had thought about aliases for a long time and she liked the sound of "Hammerseth." It was strong and lyrical at the same time. Then she remembered who she was supposed to be. "Shall we have a little prayer?"

"If it will make you feel better," Boogie said.

They had an extremely short prayer and Mary Rose turned to leave. She gave Boogie a little finger wave. "Bye, Bad Boy. I'll make sure that if I don't draw your name again, whoever does brings more of my cinnamon rolls."

Mary Rose hurried outside. The girls were at a beat-up picnic table under a big tree at the edge of the parking lot. Someone had made a coffee run because there were three Crane Coffee cups on the table in front of them. They stood up when they saw her scurry toward them. She stopped, made a gun out of her thumb and fore-finger. "Get your dumb asses into the car and don't say nothin'!"

They got their dumb asses into the Hummer and drove off. They didn't say nothin'."

Praise the Lord and Pass the Cinnamon Rolls

"Wear your Sunday-go-to-meeting hats ladies," Calamity said after Mary Rose told them about her time with Boogie Boyer. "We're going to church."

"You know who we're looking for?" Hadley asked. "You can tell just from what Mary Rose found out?"

Calamity nodded. "The most religious mob boss around is Willie Porter. He calls himself JPB for Just Plain Bill. This guy has more connections in more countries than Google. We suspected he might be the one, but JPB hasn't been active for years now." She smiled a wicked little smile. "Sooooo," she drew the word out with clown-like drama. "We go to church until we find him."

"Sweet Jesus! I mean that literally," Hadley said.

They were in Calamity's apartment, drinking coffee and munching on Mrs. Goldberg's congratulatory cinnamon rolls. Calamity's laptop sat open in front of her. She ran her fingers over the keys and waited. There was a humming sound; more keys, more humming. It was a big laptop with more keys than usual and a larger screen.

"There we go," she said, turning the computer around so they could see. Looking back at them was an attractive gentleman with graying hair, rimless glasses, a weathered, handsome face with prominent cheekbones and green eyes. He was wearing an expensive suit. The picture showed him to be well-built and trim. "Why do we always expect bad guys to look bad?" Robbie asked.

Mary Rose shook her head and smiled a sad smile. "If Boogie hadn't been so dumb, he would have been handsome. Actually, he looked a little like a bulldog puppy and I find that rather sweet." They looked at her. Then Calamity printed out a picture of Just Plain Bill for each one of them and they started talking about what to wear to church.

175

There were four churches near the location Boogie had mentioned. The first Sunday was a bust. Even though Calamity had six other agents covering the other three churches, no one spotted Willie.

"Boring," Robbie said. They were having an after-church lunch at Urban Wine in the Old Market.

Hadley smiled. "You're black. You're used to fun music and lively services," Hadley joked.
Robbie laughed. "I beg your pardon! Just because you're a 'high church' Episcopalian!" And she swatted Hadley's arm.

"I'm a recovering Catholic," Mary Rose said. "What are you, Calamity?"
Calamity looked at her. "I, my dear," she said proudly, "am a nothing."
Hadley smiled. "Robin in a pile of cow crap."

The next Sunday they chose a United Methodist

Church that advertised "Open and Welcoming."
"I think that means they have coffee and donuts,"
Hadley said.

It was a large, pleasant church, and they were
welcomed five times before they even got to the
sanctuary. Sure enough, as Hadley had predicted,
they had coffee and donuts.

"Look at the sermon," Robbie whispered to Hadley
as they settled into a pew midway down the church.
"The Five Golden Hemorrhoids and God in A Box."

"Look at the pastor's name," Hadley whispered
back, and she pointed to the bulletin. "Reverend
Doctor James M. Spasm? This is going to be good."

It was good. The Reverend Doctor Spasm was a
handsome man, close to retirement age, with thick
gray hair, a boyish smile and a thickened body. He
wore a suit, but no robe, was relaxed, and Hadley
wondered for just a second if he was married.

When it was time for the sermon, he walked out from behind the pulpit and without notes, faced his congregation and began to speak.

"God in a Box and The Five Golden Hemorrhoids," he began.

(1 Samuel Chapters 4-6)

"This story can only be told in its original earthiness
    in the words of the King James "Authorized"
version of the scriptures.
All modern translations have sanitized the scripture,
    civilized this scripture until it is acceptable and
rated G for general audience consumption.
In fact, this scripture is as close as we will ever
come to a divine obscenity."

Robbie looked at Hadley, Mary Rose looked at Calamity. They all lifted their eyebrows and looked at the preacher.

"Tumors, the modern translations say," Reverend Spasm continued. He was a good storyteller.
    "Baloney, this is not about tumors.
    It is about hemorrhoids, a devastating biological terrorist attack of hemorrhoids.

In 1 Samuel we learn the people of Israel had drifted away from God.

They had become indifferent, spiritually lukewarm.

The wicked, evil Philistines, however, are ever present in battles that never seem to end.

Whatever…the people of Israel, however devout are used to God saving them from the evil Philistines.

But not this time.

No, the evil Philistines won a battle.

The children of Israel are in shock.

What is the matter here?

This is not supposed to happen.

God is on our side.

Well, tomorrow, we should take into battle the Ark of the Covenant

The Holy box that contains the 10 commandments,

a golden jar of manna and the staff of Aaron,

a box that contains the power, the glory of God Almighty.

You know, you saw the power in that box in *Raiders of the Lost Ark*.

(well, you will never see that movie quite the same again).

With the box of the law of the Lord in their midst they can't help but win.

They have God in a box.

So they take the box into battle and lo and behold,

they not only lose another battle with the Philistines, the Philistines, steal their Holy box!

The Philistines have stolen God in a box.

They have stolen the Ark of the Covenant.

The crafty Philistines haul the power of God back to their camp and then back to the city.

They now have the power.

They were feeling very proud of themselves as they took the Ark of the Covenant into the temple of their own god called "Dagon."

That's when the problems began.

First, their statue to Dagon kept falling over. Every morning they came to the temple and Dagon was laying there with his face on the floor before the ark and by the third morning Dagon's arms had fallen off, his head was detached…this was disconcerting.

It's hard to worship a god who is falling apart and keeps falling over.

Then, after three days it seems everyone was having problems, not just the Philistine god.

There was an outbreak, no… not an outbreak, the scriptures say it was a plague…a plague of…hemorrhoids.

Imagine the discussions, probably done while standing.
They needed a solution. They needed to make it somebody else's responsibility.

Get rid of that box.

So they gave God in a box to the next town of Gath.

And pretty soon, the town of Gath who first welcomed this treasure of war was saying… 'Houston…We've got a problem.'

The epidemic of Hemorrhoids had spread to Gath.

And Lo, before you know it, this God in a Box was
a hot potato.
That's when the mayor of Gath in terrible agony
         yelled to the king in Ashsod... "Get off your
butt and do something!"

'Okay, we get it. We get it...' the King said.
'Give it back. Give God in the box back to Israel.
No... we had better do more than that.
We need to make restitution.
     We are going to have to pay them to take it back.
     And what should we give them?
When we return the box we will give them (1
Samuel 6:4 KJV)
     The likeness of Five Golden Hemorrhoids and
five Golden Rats'...
     (The rat story will have to be another sermon.)

There is a lesson to be learned from the Philistines.
     A lesson to hold and savor and never forget...
     Never, never, never,
try to capture God in a box."

They were attentive, leaning forward in their seats.

After the sermon ended, everyone applauded and

laughed. Reverend Spasm invited everyone to greet

one another. They stood. People began to hug,

laugh, and visit. Hadley turned around, smiled and

found herself shaking hands with JPB, Just Plain

Bill - Willie Porter, himself, dressed in an expensive suit and tie. His face was rugged and handsome and was topped with thick, well-styled gray hair.

"The Peace of God be with you," he said.

"And also with you," Hadley replied.

"This is my wife, Patsy," JPB said, introducing a small, trim woman dressed in an Ann Taylor top-of-the-line suit. She had dyed blonde hair and wore expensive jewelry. Hadley glanced at her fingernails. She had expected *Birthday Babe* silver after what Boogie had said. Patsy preferred a tropical coral.

"Are you visiting?" Patsy asked. Her smile was pleasant but didn't do anything for her face.

Facelift Hadley thought.

"Yes," Hadley smiled. "Do you live around here?"

Patsy nodded. "Just over on 160th. In Armbrust Acres. We're in the middle of a Cul de Sac. There's more land there and we have dogs. "

Hadley looked for Calamity. The little spy was walking quickly toward the door, moving through the crowds, talking into her big, clumsy watch.

Church had ended. They were sitting in the Hummer, watching the crowd scatter to their cars. JPB and Patsy had gotten into a white Cadillac Escalade at one corner of the parking lot.

"Are we going to tail him?" Mary Rose was excited and kept pulling at her wig. Calamity turned toward Mary Rose. "Already taken care of, but I'd like to take a look at that big mansion myself in a day or so. One last quick look before I retire."
"You're going to retire?" Robbie said.
Calamity almost smiled.

Gated Community Number Two
They were all outside at Meadow Lakes, two tables pulled together. The leaves had not started to turn but the weather was turning cooler. They sat

drinking their soft drinks, an empty plate of cinnamon rolls in front of them. An early flock of geese gaggled their way overhead, talking to each other while making their seasonal run to the south. Calamity was leaning back in her chair, hands behind her head, watching the geese. "They said upstairs that I'm too old. That if we hadn't needed to get my two bastard husbands to show themselves, they would have retired me long ago. Well, Hah! I'm as good as ever. I just need your help to cover me while I take my quick look at the Porter place."

Clyde got his two cents in. "I want to go for sure. You said they have dogs."

"Nothing ventured, nothing gained," Robert quoted, patting his holey Holy Bible.
Robbie smiled and pointed at Robert. "Peter Wastholm," they said together.
"How do you two keep doing that?" Clyde asked, exasperation squeaking out of his voice.

"Cool it, Clyde," Calamity said. Clyde cooled it and Calamity reached under the table and pulled out her laptop. "I found Porter's house on Google Earth. Come on inside. We'll work at my place."

They gathered around a table in Calamity's apartment "We're going to go look at JPB's house tonight. He and Patsy are on a weekend wine tour of Nebraska wineries. They won't be home."

"Do they really have puppies?" Clyde asked.

Calamity ignored him. "We leave as soon as it gets dark. Rest up. I want everybody bright-eyed and bushy-tailed."

"I'm going to take a nap," Mary Rose announced. "Sleep is the best gift a woman can give herself. Even Nancy Drew took naps and we are nothing if not seasoned Nancy Drews." Her energy was improving, but Mary Rose McGill was taking no chances. She didn't want to miss anything. Wiley got up and moseyed after her down the hall. Everyone left. Calamity just sat there.

Clyde headed straight for his Aunt Evangeline's apartment, and specifically toward her refrigerator. He planned to raid that refrigerator and the one in the apartment he shared with his brothers. "Puppies," he murmured to himself, and he turned it into a little song. "Here puppy, puppy, puppy. Here good, good, doggie. How much is that doggie in the window? The one with the waggily tail. Ooooh…"

Taking Down A Mansion

They were crowded into Rueben's Jesus Van again. It was even more littered and cluttered than before. No one had noticed Calamity loading her big black bag and a rope ladder into the back of the van about an hour before they left. No one had noticed Leonard helping her. As they pulled out of the circle drive, the old van backfired. Hadley squealed, Mary Rose squeaked and Robert let out a shout and held his hand over his bible.

Armbrust Acres was not only gated, it was guarded. Darkness had settled in and a soft autumn moon allowed the tree-lined entrance to lie in delicate shadows. A thin, almost skeletal guard stood up as they approached his tiny station. It reminded Robbie of an outhouse on steroids.

Rueben pulled up alongside the guard's window and Calamity climbed out of the passenger seat. She walked into the guardhouse as if she owned the place, flipped open her wallet and showed her badge. The guard was not impressed. He pointed to a clipboard, then the residences behind the gate, then at the van. He laughed. Calamity laughed with him, gave him a friendly slap on the shoulder then, in one easy move, she pulled both hands behind him, handcuffed him, and pushed him down into his chair. Before he could stand up, she

reached into her shirt pocket, pulled out a syringe
and gave him a shot in the neck.

"She's very good with syringes," Robbie said,
watching through her dirty window.

Mary Rose nodded. "I wish I could do that."

Before anyone else could say anything, Calamity hit
the button that opened the big iron gates, turned off
the lights in the guardhouse and motioned Rueben
through. As soon as the van cleared the gates,
Calamity pushed the button again and before they
could close, ran through and climbed into the van.

"That will slow'em down," she said.

Robbie's eyebrows shot up. "Slow who down?"

Here Puppy, Puppy

The Porter mansion was huge.

Robbie stared and shook her head. "Who needs this
much room?"

"Everybody who can afford it," Hadley said.

"Fear of death increases in direct proportion to
increase in wealth," Robert quoted. He was

clutching his Bible. He looked at Robbie who was looking out the window. "That was Hemingway, and he should know," he said.

Rueben had turned his lights off and was drifting as silently as the van could drift toward the big house in the center of Armbrust Acres. The neighborhood was posh, every house with perfect landscaping. Mercedes, BMWs and even Rolls Royces sat in the driveways, polished to perfection. Hadley leaned forward and whispered in Clyde's ear. "Would have been smart of us to have brought the Hummer." "Ya think?" Clyde whispered back as the Jesus Van rattled its way around the curved street.

Calamity pointed to a stand of trees near the house and Rueben bounced the van over the low curb and into theie shadows. The houses were so far apart there was little chance of being heard. Bad things could happen though if a neighbor was out walking a dog or taking a moonlit stroll. Houses on either side were dark.

Before they could jump, hop, or limp their way out of the crowed van, Leonard was at the back, helping Calamity with her oversized black bag and Rueben was wandering up the street, his hands in his jacket pocket, looking at the big house. Not only was it in a gated community, it was surrounded by an eight foot high brick wall with enough room on the wide top to lead a parade.

Robbie began to have doubts. "She said she was only going to look, right?"
Hadley nodded, "Yeah. Right."

The moon couldn't be seen through the trees, but it cast shadows on the walls and moonlight reflected off a metal design that ran around the bricks that topped the wall. Calamity moved alongside the wall until she came to a place completely concealed by the trees. It was then they noticed that she had a strong rope ladder wrapped around her shoulder.

They moved in behind Calamity, Leonard's white clothes glowing every time he stepped into the moonlight. "If anybody comes by," Robert said, "we'll send Leonard out to run at them. They'll think he's a ghost and hightail it out of here."

Calamity threw the ladder up toward the top of the wall. It slid back down. She tried again. Same thing. Rueben took it from her, stood back a few feet and let fly. It settled on top of the wall, half of it dropping neatly to the other side.

"Crap!" Calamity said. Rueben smiled. That's when they heard the dogs.

"Puppies!" Clyde yelled and he ran toward the ladder and began to scurry up it.
"Clyde!" Hadley, Robert and Robbie yelled at the same time.
"No!" Mary Rose and Wiley said together.

Leonard flapped his arms and Rueben dived toward the little man, but Clyde was on the top of the wall. There was room to stand and peer over using only reasonably good balance. Clyde was well balanced; it came with mastering walking in wedgies.

"Oh, sweet doggies!" he chimed, totally enchanted.

There was a horrendous yipping and snarling and howling. Hadley looked at Mary Rose and then at Wiley. "What kind of dogs are those?" Wiley shrugged and started moving toward the ladder.

He climbed up and joined Clyde. "Come on up," he said, turning to the group on the ground. The climb up the rope wasn't overly difficult, but it took some practice to get started up. They all crawled to the top, one by one, and sat on the wall. Yipping and growling beneath them were six fierce guard dogs.

"They're dachshunds!" Hadley was kneeling on the wall looking over at the chaos below.

"Little badger chasers," Wiley said, smiling.

"Crap!" Calamity said. Then she looked at Clyde and yelled, "Wait!" Clyde had turned and had one foot on the ladder hanging over the other side of the wall. He was going into the pack of snarling little nippers, all of them on their hind legs, front paws scratching the wall, ready for action. He was making good progress and was nearly to the ground.

"They can tear an ankle off!" Wiley yelled. Leonard flapped and both Rueben and Calamity grabbed for Clyde. They collided on top of the wall, did what looked like a strange cha-cha step and went falling headfirst into the bushes on the other side. Both went straight into all the snarls and raised hackles. Everyone on top of the wall gasped. Hadley, Mary Rose and Robbie were all on their knees now, leaning forward.

"Where's the sheriff when you need him?" Robbie said.

Hadley shrugged. "In North Dakota." And she wished for all she was worth that Wes Longbow would show up unexpectedly as he did at the grave they were robbing months before.

By this time Wiley was already half-way down the ladder, Leonard was still flapping and Robbie and Mary Rose leaned forward and looked over the wall with Hadley. What they surprised them.

Six happy doxies were crowded around Clyde, wagging their tails and eating out of his hand. One little brown dog was on his lap, licking his face. Clyde was giggling and reaching into his jacket pockets. Calamity and Rueben were getting to their feet. Twigs and pieces of bush as well as a few stray leaves hung on their clothes and in their hair. Rueben was moving his shoulder in circles and Calamity had both hands on her lower back. Wiley was standing, hands on his hips, watching Clyde and the dogs. Leonard was almost to the bottom of

the rope ladder, struggling down with Calamity's
big black bag. Robert was right behind him.

"Oh well," Robbie said. And she started down the
ladder. Hadley and Mary Rose followed and in just
minutes they were all on the manicured, seemingly
endless lawn along with six small dogs who had
fallen in love with a tender-hearted midget.

An Inside Job

"I am so too old for this shit!" Calamity said. She
looked at Robert as they started toward the house.
"That is NOT a quote,"

"I admire Jackie Chan," Robbie said. "When he
says he's too old for this shit, he means it. I hear
he's finally using stunt men now." She walked a
few steps and hopped on one foot. "Never buy new
sneakers when sneaking out at night."

"A good way to not think about your troubles is to
wear shoes that are too tight," Hadley said.

"What do we do now, Calamity?" Mary Rose asked.
She was scurrying past them to get close to their
leader. Calamity didn't answer until they got to the

front entrance. It was guarded by two gigantic stone lions. In keeping with the season, both lions wore scarves in autumn colors and had on straw hats. Pots of chrysanthemums stood by each lion.

"Exquisite taste," Robert noted.

"Nice hats," Wiley said, holding Mary Rose's hand.

Clyde had disappeared toward the back of the house, all six doxies running in circles around him, yipping happily and chasing after treats he was throwing left and right.

"Listen up!" Calamity said loudly. "I'm going to get us inside. Then we break up and look for a bottle of silver nail polish. If you find it, look on the bottom. It should look like it has a plain silver label with no writing on it. That's our chip with our agents' names and info on it. Don't mess with it, just bring me the bottle." She looked at Rueben and Robert. "Take the basement, boys."

"I want the master bedroom!" Mary Rose yelled, jumping up and down and raising her hand like a school girl. Calamity nodded.

Wiley looked at her and grinned from ear to ear. "Sounds good to me, lady."

"Okay," Calamity said, "Wiley, you're with her. Hadley and Robbie, take the kitchen and dining room. Leonard and I will take Porter's office. You have *seven minutes*, that's it. I can disable the alarm, but this sucker is state-of-the-art. It will reset itself if he coded in that he'll be gone until a certain time. After that, cops and security get here. So get up here ready to run inside and get to work."

They moved up and surrounded Calamity who took something out of the black bag and held it against the complicated lock on the front door. The moon had gone under a cloud and the night was getting cooler. Robbie leaned toward Hadley and whispered. "All we need right now is a wolf howling in the distance."

197

There was a series of clicks and the door opened. Calamity stepped inside, found the alarm box and flipped the computer-like instrument she'd used on the door so the other end was touching the alarm. More clicks.

"Okay, Go!" Calamity said. They crowded through the door which was so wide they didn't even bump into each other. Calamity and Leonard turned to the left toward large, carved mahogany doors that looked as if they could lead to an office. Hadley, Robbie, Rueben and Robert hurried to the back of the house to find the kitchen and stairs that would lead the two brothers to the basement.

"Come on, Wiley," Mary Rose said, grabbing his hand, "we have to find the bedroom."
"Music to my aging ears," Wiley said, and they hurried up a carved staircase that looked like its grandmother had been in *Gone with the Wind.*

Birthday Babe

The basement was finished and decorated with Kansas City Chiefs football team colors and décor. "No taste at all, here," Robert said.

They started lifting cushions on the ugly couch, opening drawers and doors, looking underneath a gigantic pool table in red, white and black.

In the bedroom Mary Rose stood, looking at the expensive, king-sized bed and even more expensive king-sized furniture. Wiley was pulling open drawers. "Very Victoria's Secret," he said.

Mary Rose put her finger on her chin. "I know where I'd put a bottle of Birthday Babe. I just need to think if he would put it where I think it is."

Wiley turned his head toward her. "Say what?"

"The bathroom!" and she headed into the attached his and hers bath, complete with extravagant double shower. Wiley dropped to his knees and began looking under the bed.

In the kitchen Hadley and Robbie were going through drawers, and opening cupboards. "Are we supposed to be neat about this?" Robbie asked. "I don't know," Hadley lifted an expensive pan from its hook over a center island. "I've never tossed a kitchen looking for nail polish before. This place looks like an ad for Sur la Table."

Robbie was holding a decorative candy dish painted with bright chickens. "Yo, Hadley, jackpot. Recipe cards. Here's the recipe for Herman, the cinnamon roll mix Mrs. Goldberg won't give us."
Hadley turned toward her. "Put it back, Robbie! Don't touch it. I've heard about Herman. You have to feed him all the time. He robs you of your soul. He's the demon sweet bread mix from hell. Look at Mrs. Goldberg, a slave to her Herman! As for me, I've already gained ten pounds from the cinnamon rolls and I'm not eating another one till I lose it!"

Robbie held onto the fancy recipe cards. "Hadley, that was a virtual mini-tirade. Now put on your big girl panties and check your drawers." And Robbie stuffed the recipe card deep into her jacket pocket next to Calamity's angel.

Calamity was searching through the office, handing paper files and computer discs to Leonard, who was holding Calamity's black bag open as wide as he could get it and stuffing everything she handed him inside. When he reached over and touched her arm, she jumped. He was looking up, pointing toward a chandelier and grinning. Calamity looked up. "Well, well, Leonard. Struck it rich." She pulled a chair under the big, low-hanging light and Leonard hopped up on the seat. He stretched as high as he could but couldn't reach what they were looking at. "Hold it," Calamity said, and she hurried to the chair with her arms full of big books that resembled old-fashioned encyclopedias. Leonard hopped down; Calamity set three of the books on the chair. Leonard hopped back up and stretched again. He grabbed a small white package from a crook in the chandelier. As he turned to come down, he swayed backward, lost his balance and began to fall. It was like a slow-motion movie scene. His arms went straight out, his feet went straight up, and the package flew through the air and landed softly in an overstuffed armchair. Calamity's mouth opened, her arms seemed to slowly reach for Leonard. As if there was a wind coming up from the floor, Leonard's coat blew out like a white Superman cape. He turned in mid-air, mouth open as if to yell. He landed, flat on his back, on top of Calamity.

"Crap! Crap! Crap!" The chair tipped over, the books pounded down on Calamity's head and from the big entryway beyond the mahogany doors, they could hear Mary Rose... screaming.

"I got it! I got it! I got it!" she was yelling. "We found it right where I knew it would be!" Wiley was behind her, grinning widely and glancing at his watch as he came down the curved stairs.

Leonard helped Calamity to her feet and followed her as she limped out the office door.

They all hurried into the foyer where Mary Rose was holding up a bottle of silver nail polish. *Birthday Babe!* "It was in Mrs. Porter's makeup case, just where it should be." They stood for just a second, then they all looked at their watches at the same time.

"Shhhh!" Calamity said, and she held up one hand. From somewhere in the distance came the lonely wail of sirens. "Haul ass!" Calamity yelled. They all started to rush to the door.

"Clyde!" Hadley yelled. No one had seen the little man since his wedgies had disappeared behind the house along with the doxies. Robert and Rueben looked at each other, They pushed through the crowd and rushed onto the front porch and around the house in the direction Clyde had gone with the doggies. They were hauling ass for sure.

Calamity ran off the porch dragging her black bag
which she hefted up to Leonard. He staggered a
little under its weight, then turned and flapped his
way toward the wall and the Jesus Van.

Hadley surprised herself by being in the lead to the
ladder. Calamity was bringing up the rear yelling,
"Hurry! Hurry! Hurry, damn it!" A quick thought
ran through Hadley's mind as she reached the
ladder. *She doesn't usually sound this panicked.*"

The thought vanished as she was hit in the face by a
powerful stream of water. She turned to see Rueben
and Robert running from the back of the house.
They were slipping on the grass that was being
watered by a gigantic sprinkler system. The water
was hitting them full force. Directly behind them
came Clyde, dragging a doggie travel cage filled
with five of the dachshunds. The smallest one was
tucked under his arm. The weight of the cage was
almost more than he could handle. His face was

grim and determined and he dug his wedgies into the grass in order to pull harder.

Water was pouring on the dogs from the top of the cage. Their yips had turned to whines. In just seconds another stream soaked Leonard's coat and he went scrambling after his aluminum hat that had been forced off by pure sprinkler power. Water drops sparkled in the moonlight from Calamity's white burr cut and water was running into her eyes. Wiley was making a hopeless effort to keep Mary Rose dry by holding his Stetson over her face. Robbie was looking down at her jeans, arms spread wide. She was caught running directly over a sprinkler and the entire crotch of her pants was as wet as if she'd been on a TV ad for bladder control.

"Go! Go! Go!" Calamity yelled, and after a second of stunned paralysis, the soaking friends began to move. The sirens told them the police and security units had reached the front gate where they should be rescuing the gatehouse guard about now.

Hadley surprised herself again by making it up the ladder and onto the wall first. Leonard gained ground and was right behind her, huffing and dragging Calamity's packed-full bag beside him. It was the only sound Hadley had ever heard him make.

Robbie was next, cursing lightly under her breath and holding one tight new sneaker in her hand. Hadley reached down and grabbed Mary Rose's hand and helped her up. The three women slipped and slid down the rope to the other side of the wall. There was a huge thump as Leonard tossed the bag down behind them. Rueben was carrying the cage of doxies. Clyde was worrying his way down the ladder, cradling a wet little dog in his arms, and Robert, his jacket so wet the Bible showed in his pocket, was right behind him.

Wiley was on top of the wall, reaching down to grab Calamity's hand when there was a horrendous blast and the entire estate of Just Plain Bill Porter looked as if it were an atomic bomb test site.

The sky was red. Debris was flying over their heads, landing behind them and smashing into the wall. Wiley grabbed Calamity yanked her up and fell down the ladder on top of each other.

Rueben had the back of the van open, throwing in the bag and doggie cage. Clyde had one leg entirely inside the side door and was trying to raise the rest of his body into the vehicle while still holding the little dog who was trembling in fear.

Robbie grabbed the hand hold and pulled herself up and stepped over Clyde, grabbing the little dog with one hand and Clyde's hand with the other. Hadley was right behind her. Robert, Wiley and Mary Rose tumbled in through the back. Wiley's face was covered with soot and mud, Mary Rose's slacks were muddy and torn and her beautiful wig looked like a wet dishtowel. Robert was breathing heavily and shivering, holding his soaked coat tight against his chest for warmth.

Leonard jumped in the passenger door and crawled over the center console between the front seats. Rueben slammed the doors closed and hurried behind the steering wheel. Calamity crawled into the passenger seat, and took a deep breath. She was puffing like an antique steam engine.

Hadley yelled at her. "Calamity! What on earth did you do?"

"Finished the job." Then she turned to Rueben and pointed to the jogging path just visible in front of the van. They all looked at Rueben and were completely silent. The flames from the burning house made everything as bright as day and sirens were heard now on the big circular Cul de Sac.

Rueben inserted the key into the ignition and, along with a hopeful gasp from the passengers, the old van started on the first turn.

"It's like the muggle car in the Harry Potter movie," Mary Rose said. "Always faithful."

They thumped and bumped over branches and roots, moving slowly without the lights on.

"What if we hit a tree?" Mary Rose asked.

"Or have a flat tire?" Robbie added.

"Or die from the smell?" Hadley said. "Can somebody roll down a window?"

The odor of wet dog, wet hair, wet human and smoke was overpowering. The windows were fogging over and not one of them believed the van's ventilation system would clear them off. Calamity rolled down her window and the cold air hit them like a Nordic blast. Mary Rose snuggled closer to Wiley; everyone wrapped their wet jackets tighter and moved as close together as possible. From the back of the van a sharp, single yipping started up. "Uh Oh," Clyde said. He dived over the back seat to the storage area. The van hit a root as he went over and he yelped along with the dog. Tree branches were scratching the sides of the van and they were all hanging onto each other to keep from flying out of their seats. They held on even tighter when Rueben drove as fast as he could through the fence separating the jogging trail from the gated community and the burning debris.

Only seconds has passed since they had fallen into the Jesus Van. Already all was quiet behind them. The sirens had stopped. The trail seemed to be leading them away from the danger.

"That's better," Clyde crooned. "Everything's okay now puppers." He reached over the seat. "Here, Wiley," and he handed Wiley a little dog. She was already snuggling under Wiley's chin. As she turned her little head, they could see her eyes. She was soft, brown, and obviously blind.

"Mary Rose," Clyde said, and he handed her the smallest dog, a tiny black thing, his diamond collar visible, even in the dim light of the bouncing van. Clyde was smiling and his voice was remarkably calm for the jousting they were experiencing and having just escaped a disaster. They were turning into Clyde's Doxie Rescue Team.

Calamity was leaning into the windshield, peering into the darkness. "There it is. This trail goes right under Western Avenue." In the distance they could see headlights on the major traffic artery through the city. There was a communal sigh of relief.

"All's well that ends well," Robert quoted. "Shakespeare," Robbie and Hadley said together. "Not all has ended yet, my dears," Calamity said.

But it had ended for that night. Rueben waited near the overpass above the trail and when there was no traffic, he gunned the van up the bank to the street, turned on his lights and drove slowly off as if his van was just your normal, everyday van driving down Western Avenue covered with small branches, leaves and an unusual amount of strange nature debris, all of it blowing into the street behind them. He made a turn into Scooters Coffee Shop

drive-through and ordered coffees to go. He reached
under his seat and pulled out a neatly wrapped but
somewhat squashed baggie of cinnamon rolls.

The van pulled up to a side door near Calamity's
apartment. One by one they slipped, tumbled or
climbed out. They slouched down, limped, hopped
and hurried into Meadow Lakes, hoping no one saw
them. Wiley, holding his little blind dog followed
Mary Rose who was holding her little dog and who
was following Clyde holding his little dog. Rueben
followed everyone carrying dogs and dog cage.
Calamity hurried ahead, checked to see that the
hallway was empty then unlocked and held open the
door to her apartment. She followed them inside
and turned up the heat. Rueben was shivering with
cold. He looked totally exhausted. Hadley's hair
hung in damp strands. They were dirty and tired.
They were breathing hard and removing their
jackets to better feel the heat from the furnace.
Calamity made a quick surveillance run through the
apartment, Leonard close on her heels, checking

that all blinds were shut and that no one had been there while they were gone.

"What if a whole bunch of them are hiding in here with machine guns?" Robbie said.

"Not to worry," Clyde said, "we have guard dogs."

A Brief Debriefing

They were clustered around the table in every chair Calamity could find. Rueben had lifted Clyde onto the cupboard, where he sat beside the dog cage near four sleeping doxies snuggled together into a little ball of fur. Their breathing was a soft group snore that served as calming music.

Everyone was wrapped in blankets, towels and aphgans, starting to feel warm. Calamity's bag was open on the floor; Robert's suit coat was a wadded mess at his feet and directly in the center of the table sat a small bottle of *Birthday Babe* nail polish. Calamity opened her mouth to say something and there was a loud, obnoxious ringing.

Hadley pointed. "Calamity, your watch is ringing."

"Not unexpected." Calamity looked at the watch.

"Louder than Maxwell Smart's shoe phone,"

Robbie remarked. Calamity got up and walked into

the bedroom, her watch to her ear.

Rueben was still shivering and pale. Suddenly

Calamity was at the table. "None of you were there

tonight," she said. "I did this alone."

Leonard stepped up beside her, took her hand and

motioned to himself, shaking his head. His white

coat was starting to dry but his aluminum hat was

squashed down far on his forehead. He kept

looking a Calamity, shaking his head and smiling.

Then he ran a finger over his lips. She smiled back.

"Right. You helped and you won't say anything."

She looked at the group. "Now get out of here as

fast as you can!"

It looked like a vaudeville act set to circus music.

Surprised dogs were crowded and shoved into the

cage with a couple of growls and three yelps. One yelp came from Clyde when he jumped off the counter and twisted a wedgie. Hadley, a regular Mrs. Clean, did a quick search under the sink, pulled out a can of air freshener and ran through the living room and kitchen spraying for all she was worth to kill the doggie and wet human odor. Robert, Rueben and Leonard began putting chairs back where they belonged. Wiley and Mary Rose struggled the doggie cage to the floor and began dragging it to the door. Robbie was grabbing blankets, aphgans and towels and stuffing them into the laundry hamper. They bumped into each other on their way to the door, and just as Rueben hoisted a dog cage with all six doxies packed tight and looking confused; just as Robbie, the last one out, closed the door to Calamity's apartment, they heard the sliding glass door open and a man's voice, deep and threatening say, "Agent B38?"

It was only a short way down the hall to Mary Rose's front door, but it was still early evening and residents could easily be walking between apartments, playing cards, and were likely to notice a group of damp people with bags and dogs.

They had just begun to slouch away from the danger in Calamity's apartment when Mary Rose, as loud as she could, whispered, "SHIT! Look at us. We look suspicious. Shoulders up, heads high, eyes ahead, tummies tucked in." They straightened up and walked, as casually as possible for such an entourage. They were wearing their damp jackets. Robbie's crotch was still wet, their hair was straggly and uncombed, Rueben was breathing hard and dragging the dog cage while Clyde pushed it.

They heard laughter from the card room down the hall and a soundtrack from the movie theater further up near the dining room. A lady came out of the card room, glanced at them, nodded and then walked off in the opposite direction. "There are times when you can be thankful for old eyes and poor vision," Hadley whispered.

Mary Rose scurried ahead, unlocked her door and they rushed in. The dogs began to whine but miraculously, when Clyde opened the cage and took them out, they fell silent, sniffed the air and wagged their tails. The little dog named Hershel found Rueben and walked beside him, close as possible.

They had just sat down when Wiley suddenly stood up and started digging deep into the pocket of his jeans with his right hand. "Dang, it's in here somewhere!"

"Reminds me of Mary Rose's crotch angel," Hadley said.

"Ah Ha! Look at this, short dude." He grinned at Clyde, pulled something out of his pocket that looked like a long plastic tube and tossed it to the midget. "Anybody hungry?"

"Ha!" Rueben grinned at Wiley. "A condom filled with pistachio nuts. Strange rich people."

"An unusually productive bedroom search," Robert said. "The only two things you can truly depend upon are greed and gravity." He looked fondly at

Robbie. "That greed and gravity quote happens to be one of Jack Palance's."

The little dogs were asleep on various laps and beside still-damp feet.

They looked at each other. There wasn't much to say. They were tired, still a little damp and still disheveled. They had chalked up more exercise than any of them could handle. "I have just one question," Hadley sighed. "Clyde, how did you bring all these little dogs under control? They were ready to chew us up and spit us out."

Clyde smiled. "My own secret recipe. I mixed all the hamburger I could find with all the peanut butter I could find and rolled it all into little peanutty meatballs." He reached into his jacket pocket. "I'd show you, but I don't have any left."

"Plus, he's a dog whisperer," Rueben said.

"I'm worried about Calamity and Leonard," Robbie said.

"Worrying is like a rocking chair, it gives you something to do, but it gets you nowhere." Robert said from the rocking chair. As he said it, he reached into his shirt pocket for the little Bible. When he pulled it out, the pages were stuck together from the soaking his shirt had taken. There was what looked like a wrinkled page partially poking out of the bullet hole in the front.

"You'll need a new Bible, Robert," Hadley said.

"Not on your life!" Robert said. "This one has more adventure on the outside than it does with the stories on the inside." He looked at Robbie. "That rocking chair quote? Some dude named Glenn Turner." Robbie nodded. Then she took the lead. "I'm beat and I know I won't be able to sleep after all this. I'm headed for the bathroom then bed."

She got up, went into Mary Rose's bathroom, washed her face, ran her fingers through her hair and straightened her shirt. When she came out she looked almost normal. "I recommend a bathroom trip for all of you." She hugged Mary Rose and

waited at the door while Hadley made her
bathroom trip.

"We had enough exclamation points tonight for all
the Nancy Drews combined," Hadley said as they
walked toward Robbie's apartment and the elevator
that would take Hadley to the third floor.

"We did indeed," Robbie said. She hugged Hadley
goodnight. "Think we'll ever see Calamity again?"

Robert, Rueben and Clyde left together, followed by
Wiley. "One thing about women our age," Wiley
said, "they can still be exciting."
"They're honest," Rueben said. "And they have
psychic abilities. They know all your sins before you
confess."
"As Andy Rooney said," Robert began, "For every
stunning, smart, well-coiffed, hot woman over 50,
there is a bald, paunchy relic in yellow pants
making a fool of himself with some 22-year old."
And they ambled, limped and wheezed their way
home, wondering if they would ever see Leonard, a

good brother, again and not knowing that in a short time, tragedy would strike.

Riding the Long Freight Home

The funeral was over. They had pulled two tables together once again, this time in Meadow Lake's tasteful private dining area. Robbie was seated at the end, dressed in a long black skirt and black jacket. Her grandmother's cameo brooch was on her lapel. Mary Rose sat beside her dressed in a purple dress with matching jacket. Her only jewelry was a tasteful pair of pearl earrings. Her hair had grown back in. It had sprouted in short curls, which Peyton Claireborne had assured her would disappear in time, but if she liked them, he could style her hair in that way in any shade of blonde. Right now, extremely short with soft white curls, it was very attractive. She felt good and she felt pretty again. Wiley, in a western suit with leather elbow patches sat beside her, his dress Stetson on the floor by his chair. Hadley was across the table from Mary Rose. Her black suit had a straight skirt and a strand of pearls was around her neck. Her pearl earrings, almost identical to Mary Rose's, were nestled into a gold rim in the shape of a daisy. Mrs. Goldberg was there, dressed in black, looking very different without her model's dress and daily apron. John, Meadow Lake's manager, had arranged for an over-sized chair so she could sit without oozing into her seat.

Robert and Clyde were entering the room. Robert's shoes were shined and his tie was in a perfect knot. His navy blue suit was tailored and he sported a new haircut. Clyde walked as tall as possible beside his brother, dressed in a black suit that was as close as it could come to being a tuxedo. His hair was parted and combed and while he had refused to give up his wedgie shoes, this pair was black and with his black socks, was barely noticeable.

They waited.

Their servers poured coffee into china cups and sat out trays of cheeses and meats and deli breads. In just a few minutes the door opened and Calamity came in, followed by Leonard, close on her heels.

Calamity's black pantsuit was gathered at the waist and she wore a black cotton blouse. On her lapel was a silver pin, a three and an eight nestled into the loops of the letter B, for her code name, B38.

It had been a gift from all of them after she had been forcibly retired from the agency after a firm lecture and a whine from her superiors about how she had behaved and how they had kept her on, even long after the usual retirement age. The bosses couldn't complain too much. Calamity's bag, which Leonard had stuffed full of papers and files contained valuable information about mob activities. The small package Leonard had spotted hidden in the chandelier contained a terabyte disc, the latest technology in data storage. Now the agency had all the past records of the mob, three terrorist contacts, a list of hit men and hit women, an entire list of major mobsters as well as all their birthdays. JPB Porter was loyal in sending his friends sentimental birthday cards.

Calamity's watch, a gold-plated job less than half the size of her old agency watch, was the typical retirement gift and came to about $2.59 per year of service. She pulled out the chair next to Wiley and sat down with a sigh. Her tiny Calamity angel was in her pocket as it was in the pockets of the other BOOB Girls nearly every day of their lives, even those when they climbed walls and visited hospitals.

Leonard had followed Calamity into the dining room. For the first time in the year they had known him, he wasn't dressed in white. His black suit was rented, but a good fit. His white shirt gleamed and his deflecting hat was new. He had actually removed it in the funeral home, folded it into his pocket and carried Robert's Bible for protection.

Stephanie, the Meadow Lakes concierge came by to ask if they were ready for the wine. They nodded. Wiley took a plate of meats and cheeses and breads and built a sandwich, then passed the plate around the table.

After the glasses were filled, Mrs. Goldberg rumbled to her feet. "To our Rueben," she said, her voice trembling. They raised their glasses. *"To our Rueben,"* they said together and sat down.

A tear dripped from Hadley's nose onto her sandwich. She laughed a nervous little laugh. "It never gets easier, does it? When you experience a loss, it changes your life forever. "

"Gently they go, the beautiful, the tender, the kind; Quietly they go, the intelligent, the witty, the brave. I know. But I do not approve. And I am not resigned." Robert quoted Edna St Vincent Millay.

"The worst thing about growing old," Clyde added in a rare moment of wisdom, "is facing all the deaths that come your way; the big ones, the little ones and the really huge ones, like Rueben's. Growing old is a lot like learning to ride a horse. It ends up being a pain in the butt with a whole lot of stiffness and reality every time you move."

They ate their lunch and they talked about the sweet Sasquatch who had chased Mrs. Goldberg's cat through the dining room that day months ago, who had helped them rob a grave, take down a mansion, and been a clown when Mary Rose needed clowns. They talked about the noble giant who had owned a genuine Jesus Van that now sat lonely and abandoned in a corner of the Meadow Lakes parking lot.

Three weeks after Calamity and Leonard had returned from their questioning and debriefing ordeal at Calamity's agency, Rueben had contracted pneumonia.

"Pneumonia is sometimes called 'the old man's friend,'" a young, enthusiastic doctor had told them.

"Maybe when you're all worn out and down and tired of living," Wiley had said as they stood in Rueben's room.

"Maybe when there's nothing else to do and you've been sick forever," Clyde had said, lifting Hershel onto Rueben's bed. The hospital, a progressive, friendly place, allowed pets in patient's rooms and Rueben had Hershel, the little dog he had adopted, with him every day, snuggling and sleeping and bringing smiles to everyone who came in.

But people didn't come in for long. On the third day Rueben pulled the oxygen tube out of his nose, took his Aunt Evangeline's hand in his, smiled and slipped away. Just minutes later, Hershel, the little dog who had so quickly grown close to Rueben, curled up beside his master and went to sleep forever; his nose nestled softly on his tiny paws.

"It was a wonderful eulogy, Clyde," Hadley remarked, and everyone applauded for a second time. The little man had stood in front of the podium; to stand behind it would make him seem like a disembodied voice since no one could see him. He had spoken, without notes, of his big brother's bravery, honor, honesty, and love. Clyde had pointed to the large photo on the table beside Rueben's urn, a classic picture of Rueben and Hershel, a huge man holding a tiny dog, both grinning from ear to ear.

Clyde told how his brother, with a different father, had loved little Hershel and Hershel had loved him as if they had been together since Hershel's puppyhood. "Now," Clyde had said, "Hershel and Rueben are crossing The Rainbow Bridge together, the little dog jumping, dancing, up on his hind legs with excitement, bouncing around Rueben's big feet, tiny tail a blur from wagging so fast." They had all applauded then, too.

They ate, pretty much in silence. They talked some about Rueben's van and laughed. They laughed when they remembered he wanted to be cremated because for once in his life he wanted to "think outside the box." They talked about the dogs and laughed some more. Then, as such things go, life went on. They went back to their apartments, turned on radios and televisions to take away the heavy stillness and changed their clothes.

Later that day, Robbie, Hadley and Mary Rose met at Robbie's apartment, put on their jackets, went outside to the walking trail that wound around Meadow Lakes and moved as fast as they could, their breath showing in the cold air. Calamity was nowhere to be found.

Epilogue

It had been a pretty good year.

They had rescued a diamond necklace for the BOOB Boys, loved Mary Rose through a serious illness, and loved Rueben through his death.

Mary Rose had actually gotten to get information out of a hardened criminal, even though he wasn't the smartest tattoo in the jailhouse.

A microchip had been rescued and several secret agents lives saved. The agency and FBI had the names, addresses and even birthdays of major mobsters in the area, thanks to Leonard's rescuing it from the chandelier in the mansion. Birthday cards would probably not be sent.

They had eaten way too many cinnamon rolls and were all on diets.

The dogs were very happy, each at least a pound heavier than when they went over the wall just before the mansion blew sky-high. They were part of the family at Meadow Lakes because nearly every resident had wanted one of the doxies. Rueben had his picture taken with little Hershel and the beautiful photo had adorned the alter at his funeral.

Robert fell in love with Loretta Ripp, the librarian. Having gone to the library to bone up on new quotes, Robert discovered Loretta, whose favorite books were still *Splendors of the Past* and *After the Fall,* and after buying ten copies of *Naked Librarians Calendar*, Robert invited Loretta for a glass of wine. He moved into her apartment two weeks later, taking with him five books of favorite quotes and a new Bible. Loretta became the Quote Queen of Meadow Lakes, hearing quotes from Robert, remembering them, and passing them along to all who visited her in the library.

Things were wonderfully, hopefully normal.

No one was sick, tired or run down. Thanksgiving was rapidly approaching. Hadley's grandchildren were all coming, each on a different day between Thanksgiving and Christmas. On Christmas Eve, Wes Longbow was arriving and staying until the weekend after New Year's. All of Mary Rose's daughters were coming at one time, which threatened to drive her crazy. Wiley was carefully avoiding her. It was such a day that Robbie sat alone at table 12, flyers and brochures spread in front of her.

"What's up, girl?" Hadley sat down beside her. Mary Rose joined them, a shopping list in her hand, a pen tucked into her still-curly hair.

"Look at this, you two," Robbie said, pointing to the papers spread in front of her on the table. "Ft. Robinson, the beautiful old 1873 Indian fort in the Nebraska panhandle. Just take a look," and she handed a brochure to each of them. "It's the perfect trip for next summer, an ideal time to break out the trailer and the Hummer. They've done nothing all year but gather dust. And we have months to plan and dream about a trip such as this."

Hadley looked at her brochure. "I know Ft. Rob," she said, waving the paper in front of her. "Crazy Horse was killed there."

"I'd go right now if I could," Mary Rose sighed. "It's beautiful, it's historic, they have all kinds of activities and I bet Calamity would have a fit. We can ride horses and sight-see and she could be a real clown if there's a rodeo around."

"Speaking of Calamity," Mary Rose said, "have you seen her since dinner last night?" The little spy had not shown up for breakfast and now it was mid-morning. They turned as Jane and John, the managers, walked through the door. Robert was beside them and Clyde was hopping along behind them, talking loudly and waving what looked like a note. Jane held an identical note in her hand and was nodding at whatever Clyde was saying. They hurried to table 12.

"Look at this!" Clyde said, "Just look at this!" He waved the note then threw it down in front of Hadley. Jane handed the second note to Robbie. "I imagine they're identical," she said. Robbie unfolded the note, written on a plain sheet of computer paper.

Leonard and I have run away to join the circus, she read. She looked at Hadley who was picking up the paper Clyde had thrown down in front of her.

Calamity and I have run away to join the circus, Hadley read aloud. She turned the note around so they could all see. Leonard had made a sketch which looked remarkably like Stephen King's Pennywise the evil demon clown.

They were totally quiet, looking at the notes. All at once Clyde grinned and began to laugh. "Hot damn!" he said. "They ran away to join the circus!"

"Calamity is going home," Hadley said, smiling.

"And Leonard will fit right in," Mary Rose added.

"What a retirement!" Robbie said, "What a team."

"Let us never be too old to dream the dreams of adventure," Robert said.

Robbie looked at him for the source of the quote. "Joy Johnson," he said.
"Oh my gosh, is she still alive?"
"I understand she's spending time in Ft. Robinson in western Nebraska, researching her next book."

"We'll miss Calamity and Leonard." Hadley smiled a sad smile. Robert and Clyde pulled up chairs. A Meadow Lakes server came over with a pot of decaf coffee in one hand and a pot of regular in the other. "She never quite fit in," she continued.

Robbie picked up the conversation. "I think her life was too different, too isolated and secret. And like Mrs. Goldberg said, she didn't have our history. She probably gave us all she could and more than most people would get from her."

Mary Rose reached into her pocket and pulled out her Calamity Angel, kissed it and put it back. "What a time we had together!" Clyde said.

"Andy Rooney says once you get past the wrinkles, women over fifty are more beautiful and sexy than younger ones," Robert said. "You are all well past fifty, tremendously beautiful and it is a delight just knowing you. Missing Calamity and meeting Loretta causes me to be sharply aware of that."
"He's smitten," Hadley said.
Robbie nodded. "Dead meat."
"Hopeless," Mary Rose said.

Hadley stood up, "Okay girls, let's do the pose. Maybe we can find a way to send it to Calamity and Leonard." She stood, hands on hips, chin held high, one arm raised as if holding a gun. Robbie jumped up and stood in front of her and on her left in a side view, right armed raised, fingers forming a gun as well. Mary Rose struck the identical position facing the opposite direction. There they were. Kelly, Jill and Sabrina. For all it was worth, they looked very little like Farah Fawcett, Jaclyn Smith or Kate Jackson. Robert got out his Android cell phone and snapped two pictures, one after the other. Clyde did a reasonable imitation of John Forsythe. "Well done, Angels. You are beautiful. Now go enjoy yourselves."

"Thank you, Charlie," the three angels said.

"Speaking of beautiful," Clyde said, and he nudged Robert and made a motion with his head toward the middle of the room.

Coming toward them was a tall, stately woman more colorful than any they had seen since Mrs. Goldberg had combined her purple apron with her red model's coat and pink crotched slippers. This woman didn't walk, she floated. Her hair was long and dyed a deep black. She wore a blue shirt under a purple jacket and her skirt, which fell in graceful folds around her ankles, was multicolored with specks of unidentified sparkles throughout. Her boots, showing tastefully beneath her skirt were bright red. Her belt was wide and gold. There were bangles on her wrists, gold chains around her neck and gold loops hanging from her ears. She was coming directly toward them. They were staring at her unashamedly. Hadley's mouth was hanging slightly open and when she realized it, she swallowed hard and closed it tight. Robbie realized her hand was still imitating a revolver and lowered it. Mary Rose kept her pose and stared.

"Allo," the woman said, moving close in beside Robert. There was a faint and unusually pleasant spicy scent emanating from her wrists and throat and probably her breasts as well. "I am Esmeralda St Benedict and zee manager said I should come yere to see eef I may join you." She had a soft Romanian accent. Robert stood and offered her his chair. Clyde stood as well and looked as if he might melt into the carpet. Esmeralda St Benedict smiled at him and Clyde did melt. She bent her head toward Robert who actually bowed. She looked at the other three women and smiled even wider. "A most attractive pose. Charlie's Angels?" She had beautiful teeth. They stared at her. She was tall and gorgeous. She looked at Robbie then Hadley then Mary Rose, nodding a friendly nod at each BOOB Girl.

"I yam gypsy," she said.

And she sat down, crossed her shapely legs and winked at Clyde.

Mrs. Goldberg's Cinnamon Rolls

Warning: this is the starter and recipe for Herman, also known as Amish Friendship Bread. It is to be baked, tended, loved and given away. Be aware that if you continue with this delicious recipe, it will drive you up a wall, as Hadley has already warned us. You have to keep enlarging it, stirring it, adding to it and giving it away. Friends eventually will no longer invite you over because they know you will be bringing Herman. They've already lost most of their friends by giving them Herman week after week. This is the real reason Mrs. Goldberg spent so much time in her kitchen. She was trying to use up all of Herman.

Brad, the chef at Meadow Lakes had a better idea. He UPS'ed starter to every chef in the Omaha telephone directory and never included a note OR his return address. There is still confusion in major kitchens in the city to this day.

Herman the Amish Friendship Bread Starter
Mrs. Goldberg's Secret Cinnamon Rolls Recipe

(Note from Joy) This was found for me by my friend of 40 years, Mary Vondra who is definitely related to Wiley and who laughed when I asked her for it because she knows what's going to happen to you once you make it.

Starter:
2 pkg. active dry yeast
1/4 c. warm water
1 c. flour
1 c. sugar
1 c. warm milk (110 degrees)
Making the starter:

1. In a small bowl, dissolve the yeast in warm water for about 10 minutes. Stir well.

2. In a 2 quart glass or plastic container, combine 1 cup sifted flour and 1 cup sugar. Mix thoroughly or the flour will get lumpy when you add the milk.

3. Slowly stir in warm milk and dissolved yeast mixture. Loosely cover the mixture with a lid or plastic wrap. The mixture will get bubbly. Consider this Day 1 of the cycle, or the day you receive the starter.

For the next 10 days handle starter according to the instructions for

Amish Friendship Bread or Herman

Note: Never use anything but wooden or plastic spoons, wooden, porcelain or plastic bowls. Never use anything metal. Already you can see how bossy this recipe is. Now you're going to mix it up, bake it, feed it and leave it out on your kitchen cupboard to do Stephen King-like things in your kitchen while you sleep at night. This is *before* you begin to alienate your friends.

Day 1.....This is the day the bread is baked (or day 10) If you received your starter today, do nothing. It has already been stirred. Transfer to a wider container if it rises close to the top

DO NOT REFRIGERATE!!!!!!!!!!!! (ever!)

Day 2, 3, 4........Stir
Day 5......Add 1 cup flour, I cup granulated sugar, 1 cup milk
Day 6, 7, 8, 9......Stir
Day 10....Add 1 cup flour, 1 cup granulated sugar,1 cup milk.

Pour 1 cup of the mixture in each of three containers. This is now the new starter. Give 2 of these with instructions to friends and keep one for yourself.

Cinnamon Rolls

2 cup flour
1 cup milk
1 cup Amish Friendship Bread batter (previous page)
1 egg
3 tsp sugar
1/2 cup shortening
1 tsp salt
1/2 tsp baking soda
1 tsp baking powder
1/4 cup sugar
1 tsp cinnamon
1/2 cup crushed nuts

Combine flour, milk and Amish batter and let set at room temperature overnight or 10-12 hours. Stir down. In a separate bowl, mix egg, 3 tsp. sugar, shortening, salt, baking soda and baking powder. Add to batter mixture and stir down. Pour dough out on well floured board and knead until no longer sticky. Roll out onto 1/2" thickness in a rectangle shape. Brush dough with soft butter. Mix together 1/4 cup sugar, cinnamon and crushed nuts. Sprinkle cinnamon-sugar mixture over buttered dough. Beginning at wide side, roll up, and seal seam. Cut 1" slices and place on well greased cookie sheets. Let rise 30 minutes. Bake at 350 degrees F 30-35 minutes.

When cool, frost by mixing

1 c. powdered sugar
1 tbsp. milk
1/2 tsp. vanilla or other flavoring

Mrs. Goldberg was fond of adding almonds, raisins softened by soaking in water for 10 minutes,, pecans and other nuts and sweet things. Luckily for us there are tremendous Herman recipes on the internet. Google away happily.

Eat Live Love Enjoy
Read and Adventure on!

Thanks, Appreciation and Downright Gratitude
I do not know who created the Four Great Religious Truths,
but if I ever find out I'll buy the ice cream or the coffee or the
wine. It's my favorite joke and came from a surrogate son,
Patrick Davis, who at that time was director of Chaplaincy
for Alegent Health in Omaha. Patrick sent it when I requested
jokes for my uterine cancer surgery years ago now.

A simple hug and thanks for my lifetime friend, **Dr. Robert
Dodder**, retired United Methodist Minister (if ministers ever
really retire) who let me model Robert after him in appearance
and profession. And to my other lifetime friend and psychic
connection, my classmate - Just Plain Bill, **Dr. William
Porter** who is anything but plain.

There really is a Bear Family and a real Bear Cemetery.
Thanks to the real **Ted Bear and Bryce Bear** and to the
Bears, who happen to be *my* family.

Thanks to the **Rev. Dr. James A. Campbell**, also known as
"Slick Sheetz" who donated the delightful sermon of God in A
Box and Five Golden Hemorrhoids. Jim is the author of good
books on theology, humor and humanity.

Thanks to friend and colleague **Darcie Sims** for the "When
have you heard someone say 'I'm stressed, let's go have
salad'" quote.

A condom full of pistachio nuts to **Kathy Tooker**, my Boob
Girl Buddy and head of the Eastern Nebraska Library
Association who deserves a hug and a high five for the Naked
Librarians Calendar.

A glass of good chardonnay to **Dr. Deb Romberger, Dr.
Carol Beaty and Rev. Stephanie Ahlschwede**; their own set
of BOOB Girls.

For two of my most interesting lunches of the year I thank the
real Warden and officers; Warden **Karen Shortridge,** and
Teresa and Loretta who gave us a view into a really well-run

men's prison and to **Nancy Hemesath,** good buddy and outstanding Executive Director of Ted E. Bear Hollow.

For the Herman recipe we can all be grateful to **Mary Vondra** (definitely related to Wiley.

Kathy McNamara not only took the flattering photo of Barney and me on the back cover, but is a good friend and good promoter and after working 25 years for the IRS could put Calamity to shame.

To all the BOOB Girls at **The Bookworm,** for research and the best book signings ever, and to **Stanley Hill** and everyone who gave me ideas and stirred my imagination, a new bookmark and appreciation to all of you.

A whole lot of red soup bowls from the dollar store to **Rita Hurlbutt** and her Red Hat Smooties Dance Troup. Rita actually did make a bedpan hat. Some women just have better ideas.

To my BOOB Girl consultants, **Carol, Dianna, Lucy, Nancy, Connie and Mark, Kathy and Mike, Andrea, Louise** and especially to my main supporters: my husband **Marv,** my daughter and writing partner, **Jenny Ritter** and my daughter, **Janet,** Executive Director of Centering Corporation – I love all of you.

Thanks to my proof readers, my sweet Marv, and Marc Roberts, who is also sweet. Any typos you find in this book were left there by Marv and Marc for your amusement.

About the Author

Joy Johnson is 76 now. With her husband, Dr. Marvin Johnson she co-founded Centering Corporation, North America's oldest and largest bereavement resource center and Ted E. Bear Hollow, Omaha's center for grieving children. She is a nationally-known speaker and has written or edited over 100 books on grief, mostly for children.

Joy's husband, Marv, died this year. However, Joy's three children, Jim, Jenny and Janet, all live near her in Omaha as do her six grandchildren, Jessica Joy, Paris Jennifer, Alex, Emma, Gregory and Liesel. Barney the Bernese Mt Dog is too big for her retirement community and lives now with Janet and Ben from Centering Corporation. Joy is at home with and loves a fat tabby cat named Margaret Thatcher.

If you enjoy this book, you'll love and laugh with:

The Boob Girls:
The Burned Out Broads at Table 12

The Boob Girls II:
Lies, Spies and Cinnamon Roles

The Boob Girls III:
Sandhills and Shadows

The Boob Girls IV:
Murder at Meadow Lakes

The Boob Girls V:
The Secret of the Red Cane

www.theboobgirls.com